MIKE LANCASTER

EGMONT

EGMONT

We bring stories to life

1.4 first published in Great Britain 2012
by Egmont UK Limited
239 Kensington High Street
London W8 6SA

Text copyright © Mike Lancaster 2012

The moral rights of the author have been asserted

ISBN 978 1 4052 5818 0

1 3 5 7 9 10 8 6 4 2

A CIP catalogue record for this title is available from the British
Library

Typeset by Avon DataSet Ltd, Bidford on Avon, Warwickshire

Printed and bound in Great Britain by the CPI Group

48752/1

EGMONT

Our story began over a century ago, when seventeen-year-old
Egmont Harald Petersen found a coin in the street. He was on
his way to buy a flyswatter, a small hand-operated printing
machine that he then set up in his tiny apartment.

The coin brought him such good luck that today Egmont has
offices in over 30 countries around the world. And that lucky
coin is still kept at the company's head offices in Denmark.

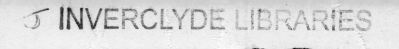
The future isn't what it used to be.

Yogi Berra

For Fran, for ever
For Claudia, Meryl and Sofia, for reading
And for Becky and Philippa, for helping

And in loving memory of:
Andrew Paul Lancaster 1964–1995
Joan Mary Henson 1938–2010

Contents

Nearly a thousand years have passed since
the recording of the Straker Tapes . . .

Heisenberg University

Professor Lucas Whybrow
Professor of WorldBrain Studies

The story of Peter Vincent might easily have never been heard. Indeed, it was by pure accident that the flash-memory drive, containing the files and fragments that make up his story, was absorbed into the WorldBrainMass.

The brain's annual growth plan meant that new areas of its underground complex were being claimed as sites for further expansion. These areas, or 'rooms', were flooded with nutrients and new BrainLobes seeded on to them.

Janitor's logs show that the new areas set aside for lobe growth were not properly checked.

I believe that, during brain expansion, the data storage unit was absorbed by the young BrainLobes and converted into food, and that Peter Vincent's data entered the BrainMass as a side effect of this process.

I discovered the data, also accidentally. While checking

file systems, I came across sectors that seemed out of place and worked for several days to isolate the data; then spent four months rebuilding them into a file system that I could read.

Corrupt data was then analysed and has been carefully reconstructed using markers I discovered within the Vincent files themselves.

I am satisfied that the Vincent data I am presenting now is as accurate as it is humanly possibly to recreate. I have even included fragments – which are in the form of lists that Peter Vincent seemed to like making.

In this record, Peter Vincent speaks of a world that once was and tells a startling story that seems to contain answers to many of the questions we routinely ask ourselves as human beings. It is also flawed and contains errors and gaps that will only open Peter Vincent's story to accusations of fraud and dishonesty.

I will, however, leave you to be the judge.

RECOVERED SECTORS/
File-set 1

'The First Day of My Last Days'

*In extraordinary times, the ordinary takes
on a glow and wonder all of its own.*

Kyle Straker

prologue

File: *224/09/12fin*

Source: *LinkData\LinkDiary\Live\Peter_Vincent\Personal*

<RUN>

. . . Alpha . . .

. . . I want to tell her that I'm sorry, tell her something for hex sake . . . but the world is ending and this . . . this is all I have left.

All we have left.

It . . . I . . . this has all gone badly wrong.

We are deep underground in these chambers beneath the world we know . . . thought we knew . . . beneath the city and I . . .

I guess I thought that we had a chance . . . Alpha and me . . . that everything that has happened could still have a

4

happy ending, like in the stories my mother used to tell me.

It's weird.

I've been thinking about my mother a lot in the last couple of days. Before all of this, I think I would have found it almost impossible to remember what she looked like without consulting my LinkDiary; now I can see her in my mind plainly, I can remember the sound of her voice as if I was still hearing it.

I remember . . .

<. . . There is a shimmer, like a mirage, a trick of the light, and I am momentarily blinded.

By the time my vision clears, my mother is gone . . .>

Oh.

I'm letting my mind run away with me again, and I haven't got time to let it do that. That's one of the problems with playing around with memories, the wrong ones can bubble up and come into focus at the wrong moment.

I don't even know if that's the actual memory, or my memory of examining that scene later . . . but now I'm really *getting ahead of myself.*

I don't know if this will be my last diary entry.

I guess it probably will be.

So I need to put a copy of my diary on to an external memory source, because people . . . people need to know. They have to be told. Reminded. Whatever.

I'm having to edit the relevant memory files on the fly; to concentrate on the parts of my daily record that will show the world the truth.

We are in a room full of boxes of useless stuff: relics and papers and an ancient flash drive that I have repaired with my filaments – it should be able to store this data, but I will have to compress the information to fit the limitations of the drive.

I'm sitting here, in the near dark, and I should be talking to Alpha, or holding her, or something like that – but instead I'm hacking into my own memories and editing and copy and pasting, all with my heart beating out of control in my chest while she watches on.

So this is fear. I have to say, I can see why we have strived to eradicate it from our lives.

I'll start shunting the parts I've done on to the memory drive.

The first diary entries – I can't believe it was only three days ago.

Three days?

It feels like a lifetime.

The world has changed . . . is changing . . . and I am the only one who can make a record of the truth.

Here we go . . .

>Deploying filaments . . . <

<DUMP MEMORY>

-1-

File: *113/42/00/fgh*

Source: *LinkData\LinkDiary\Peter_Vincent\Personal*

<LinkDiary On>

I know that I have been talking about it for weeks, but today I actually went ahead and did it.

I signed up for Professor King's class.

Next semester I'm going to be studying English literature. I've even got a reading list to prove it.

Which gives me maybe a month or so to pluck up the courage to tell my father.

Perry came along to offer me moral support. He started grinning when I used my filaments to sign up to the class's register, and he's been grinning at me ever since. His mouth is so unused to any kind of smile that it's not a pretty sight.

'Peter, Peter, Peter,' he said. 'I know you're going through a mid-teen crisis, but what do you think your dad's going to say about this, eh?'

I shrugged. 'He'll call a medic,' I said. 'His only son is going to be reading books that – for once – *don't* try to explain the secrets of life, the universe and everything. He'll probably blame it on a virus.'

'You know, literature *can* be seen as an attempt to explain those same secrets,' Perry said. He pretty much has a clever answer for every occasion.

'Yeah, right,' I replied. 'What's that I can hear?' I cupped my ear with my hand. 'Oh, it must be my father's laughter ringing around the house when I try that line on him.'

Perry spent a couple of seconds thinking.

The effort made his face scrunch up.

'Well,' he said, finally, 'I guess the last line of defence is that it *is* an extra class ...'

'Oh Perry,' I said. 'My wonderful, water-brained friend. That's not going to make him feel any better about it, is it? Not only am I taking a soft subject, but I'm also wasting the time I *could* be using for extra science studies to do it.'

Perry grinned again. Wider, if that was possible.

'Oh well,' he said, 'You're doomed.'

'I know.' I matched his grin. 'Fun, isn't it?'

Perry slapped me on the shoulder way too hard.

In truth it had been his enthusiasm for Professor King's classes that made me want to sign up in the first place.

Perry Knight is one of those people who rarely displays any kind of emotion, managing to keep cool at all times. And he has a terribly serious face that makes him look like he's picking up constant bad news from the Link.

Hearing him enthusing about the books that Professor King was getting him to read — and watching his face light up with sheer excitement when telling me about it — well, it made me want to see what in the world it was that had got him so animated.

Plus — and I know my dad wouldn't like this, but it's true — I'm getting a bit sick of science textbooks.

Actually:

<LinkEdit\Encrypt that last sentence\My eyes only>

In fact:

<LinkEdit\Encrypt entire diary\My eyes only>

Can't be too careful.

The student lounge was usually a buzzing mass of students, but today Perry and I had the place to ourselves. It was supposed to be a free period, but the college had suddenly, and quite unexpectedly, raised the learning quota a couple of days ago and the empty room was evidence that everyone else was playing catch-up; desperately trying to earn more edu-credits before the big Student Audit next week.

Perry and I were already *way* above its threshold.

That's why we could afford to be sitting around while everyone else panicked.

I'm not as crazy bright as Perry, but I reckon I'm not far off. We breezed through pre-prep, prep and then school together, and ended up at the same college in New Cambridge because it was the best. And so were we.

It might sound like bragging, but it's true.

When you're the son of someone like David Vincent, it's the very least that's expected of you.

Of course, Perry's father works for my father, so we've been friends since we were old enough to, like, *have* friends.

We're as close as brothers would have been in the old days, before the population explosion led to the One Child Limit on family sizes.

We are both supposed to follow in our fathers' footsteps and end up in the very same labs where they work.

Supposed to.

If we don't let Professor King's Literature class knock us from the path our fathers have so carefully built for us.

<LinkDiary Off>

Professor King

2nd Semester Reading List

1. Gulliver's Travels

tags: <Swift> <satire> <adventure> <politics>
<knowledge vs. wisdom> <religion>

2. Romeo and Juliet

tags: <Shakespeare> <play> <romance> <fate> <violence>

3. Wordsworth: Selected Poetry

tags: <Wordsworth> <poetry> <nature> <memory>

4. Great Expectations

tags: <Dickens> <Victorian> <social realism> <crime>
<class>

5. Ronnie Barker: Collected Works

tags: <Barker> <humour> <20th century> <four candles>

6. Heart of Darkness

tags: <Conrad> <colonisation> <madness> <human greed>
<evil>

7. The Maltese Falcon

tags: <Chandler> <crime> <class> <betrayal>

8. Midnight's Children

tags: <Rushdie> <memory> <the one vs. the many>

9. Flanimals

tags: <Gervais> <cryptozoology>

10. Sense and Sensibility

tags: <Austen> <marriage> <appearance vs. reality>
<jealousy>

11. Beowulf

tags: <anon.> <heroism> <violence>

12. 0.4

tags: <Straker> <Strakerite> <fantasy> <satire>

<religion>

-2-

File: *113/43/00/fgi*

Source: *LinkData\LinkDiary\Peter_Vincent\Personal*

<LinkDiary On>

I almost told my father last night.

I mean: if he had come home I would have. Probably.

But he pushed me a message saying he was stuck at the lab, and it didn't feel right talking about it over the Link, so another day passed by without me mentioning it.

I ended up spending most of the evening reading an actual book on my LinkPad. The process of reading a book takes a while to get used to. It's so slow and laborious. But once you get into it, once you forget the way you're reading and concentrate on *what* you're reading, it becomes a really unique experience. You have to work to draw meaning from it rather than having a meaning given to you, which is the only way we receive information these days.

It doesn't tell you how to think.

The book is called *Gulliver's Travels* and it's about this sailor who keeps ending up in weird situations in even weirder countries. It's pretty funny, but in a way that makes you wonder about life and stuff, and it got me thinking about how we put our trust in people who probably don't actually deserve it.

The weird thing is, it kept me off the GameServers for the whole evening.

I realised that I would *like* to discuss it in class: so many things in it kept popping back into my mind.

My father would hate it. 'Waste of time and energy' he'd call it.

And this morning he was just too busy to be interrupted. He's always thinking and theorising, and he often forgets that a son needs a little . . . I don't know . . . *parenting*, I guess. It might be nice to be asked how things are going at college, or in my life, but my father never thinks these things are worth talking about. He lives in his own head, and his body is just a machine that his brain uses to get from place to place.

He has a lab in the house, in case of domestic eureka moments. Not that I have ever been allowed to see it: I am so irrelevant to him that he's never even let me. And I'm so scared of his disapproval that I've never dared look inside when he's not here. How sad is that?

He expects me to be just like him, too, but I'm not. Not really. I don't like to think all of the time. Sometimes I actively *avoid* thinking: logging myself on to one of the many GameServers and losing myself in a Digital Environment.

The world seems *too full* sometimes, with so much information that it gets hard to see past it all. You can get lost in data and newsfeeds and SocNetworking and forget that there's a real world out there, buried beneath all that information.

That's why the book surprised me.

It was talking about an ancient world, but it actually made me think about this one: about the silly things we do as a kind of reflex action, without giving them a second thought.

Breakfast was spent in silence, with my father frowning at the problem consuming his attention, and I almost interrupted his train of thought just to get him to look at me.

Or speak to me. If only to tell me off — that would have been OK.

But I ate my high calcium breakfast quietly instead.

And then I took a slider to college and tried to remember when I started keeping secrets from my father.

The problem is that the longer I leave it, the harder it gets to tell him. And he's not easy to talk to at the best of times.

<LinkDiary Off>

-3-

File: *113/43/00/fgj*

Source: *LinkData\LinkDiary\Peter_Vincent\Personal*

<LinkDiary On>

My life is getting weird.

Like I've opened some strange door by signing up for an extra class, and now other things are coming out through that door.

Like Amalfi.

Amalfi Del Rey.

I guess the Amalfi thing only happened because Ms Donlevy embarrassed me in front of the class.

In fairness she probably didn't mean to, but when she started talking about my father in glowing, reverential tones it made my face redden, nevertheless.

My father casts a long, long shadow, even across my science lessons.

We were discussing the development of artificial life, and Ms Donlevy decided to illustrate the talk with an infoslice on David Vincent's breakthrough work on the bee project.

Bee numbers had been declining for centuries, and careful study of environmental factors had at least stabilised them for fifty or so years.

But then the Black Labium mite arrived. The mite was a parasite, and it was small enough to make its home on the feeding tubes of honeybees.

Generally speaking, parasites maintain a balance with their hosts: they take a little of what they need, without putting their host in danger. This makes sense: killing a host is pretty bad business for a parasite.

Unfortunately, the black mites had crossed over from another threatened species – a butterfly, of all things – and they were ignorant of the needs of honeybees. They prevented the bees from receiving some amino acids that they needed to survive.

And the extinction of the bee as a species began in earnest.

The problem with losing the bees was that the plants they worked so hard to fertilise also came under the threat of extinction. And without plants, the human race would face a very bleak future indeed.

At the time, my father had been a researcher on an artificial life project that had already engineered an electric ant. Artificial creatures were a relatively new area of study, but there had been a few successes. What made my father's ant different from the dozen or so other living robots was its ability to think.

And it was a triumph of miniaturisation: where some of the other creatures were unwieldy and large, my father's electric ant was just about the same size as the real thing.

When it was forecast that honeybees would be totally extinct within ten years, my father's team had turned their attentions to the creation of *artificial* honeybees.

I remember my father telling me that they had attempted to copy the precise structure of the creature they were trying to mimic. But it had turned out to be a dead end because it was so hard to get the bees to fly as accurately and delicately as they needed.

So, eventually, they had ditched the natural template and went for a design that looked nothing like a bee at all. In fact it owed its form more to the common housefly, with some pouches added to its backmost pair of legs.

The infoslice that Ms Donlevy showed even had a vid of my father addressing a symposium.

'Programming the bees was the easy bit,' he said from the vid. 'Making them weatherproof was the real challenge.'

After a few prototypes had been built, the artificial bees had gone into mass production and were released into the wild with huge success. All the plants of the world had been saved, and my father was guaranteed a lifetime of wealth.

You see, the bees couldn't reproduce — and they had a pretty limited lifespan — which meant that they were always in demand.

And always in production.

Ms Donlevy suddenly turned to me. 'Your father is an incredible man,' she said, 'and an inspiration to us all.'

I fashioned a passable smile and then looked around.

Everyone in the room, it seemed, was staring at me with smirks and sneers on their faces. And that only made my face feel hotter.

Even Perry had his eyes raised to the ceiling in mock exasperation.

Thanks Perry, I thought, *never mind that your father helped too.*

I honestly didn't know where to look. And, in searching for a place to rest my eyes, I saw a female face that was studying me with something different in her expression.

Warmth. Maybe compassion?

I hadn't seen her before, but I appreciated her look and gave her an uneasy smile.

She smiled back at me and then turned her attention to Ms Donlevy at the front of the room.

'I can't help thinking that it might have been better if he'd targeted the mites instead of the bees,' the girl said pretty loudly.

Ms Donlevy's face did three things in quick succession: it stretched with shock, then crinkled with puzzlement, before relaxing into amusement.

'Ah, Miss . . . *Del Rey*, I believe.' Ms Donlevy spoke with the kind of fake brightness that was so shallow you could hear the steel reinforcements running under the surface of her words. 'Would you care to elaborate on that point for the benefit of the rest of us?'

The girl nodded enthusiastically.

'I was just thinking about the Law of Unintended Consequences,' she said brightly. 'David Vincent's work was visionary, but he approached the problem from the point of view of an engineer. He manufactured an artificial bee that saved the world . . .'

'I'm struggling to see a problem here.' Ms Donlevy's voice became that little bit sharper.

'Well, have you seen any real bees lately?' the girl said. 'Of course you haven't. The fake bees were so good at their job that they muscled out the biological ones. We didn't save them, we simply engineered their replacements.'

'Replacements that saved the world's food crops,' Ms Donlevy said, crossing her arms.

I was sitting there watching, shocked.

I mean no one talks to Ms Donlevy like that. She's one of

our more . . . *formidable* lecturers. She can cut frivolous or disruptive students down with nothing more than a look.

But I also felt a little bit of admiration. The girl might be arguing at the expense of my father, but you had to admit: she *did* have a point.

'I'm only suggesting that if we had focused our energies on attacking the mites we could have saved the real bees,' the girl said matter-of-factly.

'The word "could" is key in your observation,' Ms Donlevy said coldly. 'And as much as I enjoy a game of "if only we had", this is neither the time nor the place to indulge in such pursuits. I realise that you are new here, Miss Del Rey, so I will suggest to you that you keep your asides to yourself in future. Now if you could all open up your LinkPads . . .'

It wasn't as bad a smacking down as Ms Donlevy could have delivered, and I saw the faintest of smiles pass across Miss Del Rey's lips when our eyes met.

LinkList/Peter_Vincent

My Top 5 LinkTunes Playlist

5.

'My Quantum Beatbox' by The Definite Articles

A thumping slice of techno mayhem, with the vocals sampled from a children's educational film about quantum jumps. Contains equations for the calculation of quantum events, but they never get in the way of the music. And the drum programmer isn't just keeping time on this track, he's inventing it.

My Rating: **

4.

'If I Dream' by Mr Melt

An orchestral opening gives way to some fierce industrial guitars in this cover version of an old Eddie Leakey choon. But where the original was about the courage of dreaming the impossible, Mr Melt subverts the message with subliminal tones that evoke nightmares. Powerful stuff.

My Rating: ****

3.

'Until the Sun Goes Cold' by Laurie Lauren

A smooth, chilled-out ballad. OK, it's about the eventual cooling down of the sun, but it's not as gloomy as that might make it sound. Laurie's voice stretches through the octaves, but it's in a less showy way than on her last few tracks. 'The last winter ever / Temperatures are falling / Hello Hello / Eternity is calling.'

My Rating: ****1/2

2.

'Lumpy Gravy' by A Clinical Sign

Apparently another cover, but the original exists only on paper and hasn't been heard for many centuries. A Clinical Sign are forging a bit of a niche for themselves by recording songs from so long ago, but it sounds fresh and new and as if it was written yesterday.

My Rating: ****3/4

1.

'Forward, Only Forward' by The Little Engines of Destruction

Every now and then a song comes along that manages to condense thousands of years of civilisation into one seven-minute dance track. DogFather's 'This Is Where We're From' started the trend, but TLEofD's title track from their new compilation encyclopaedia takes the idea and runs with it.

At times the compressed historical information is a little overwhelming, even disorientating, but I feel that was kind of the point. And, let's face it, it's a great way to learn.

My Rating: *****

-4-

File: *113/43/00/fgj/Continued*

Source: *LinkData\LinkDiary\Peter_Vincent\Personal*

<LinkDiary Running>

Mercifully the lesson ended pretty soon after.

The rest of the class were filing out of the lecture hall, but I'd remained seated, waiting for the room to empty.

'Look, I'm sorry about my outburst,' said a voice at my shoulder. 'But she really shouldn't have done that.'

I turned around and was surprised to see Miss Del Rey. She was blonde, with piercing blue eyes and a mouth that looked mischievous.

I avoided turning bright red and managed to reply, 'Who shouldn't have done what now?'

'Ms Donlevy, putting you on the spot like that. It wasn't fair.'

'I guess that's the problem with following in the footsteps of someone with massive feet,' I said, trying to sound dry and witty. 'Or living in the shadow of a monolith. Choose your preferred metaphor.'

'I think I'll go for metaphor A,' she said. 'You're Peter, right? I'm Alpha.'

'Alpha?' I asked her.

It was Alpha's turn to look uncomfortable.

'It's better than Amalfi,' she said. 'That's me, by the way. Amalfi Del Rey.' She smiled a thin smile. 'My parents didn't seem to realise that a name has to be said out loud.'

I packed my LinkPad into my bag and zipped it up.

'Anyway, I'm sorry. Attacking your father; it was out of line.'

I think I surprised her by smiling. 'It was an interesting point you were making. And to be honest it was worth it just to see Ms Donlevy's face. It's good to meet you, Alpha.'

'Good to meet you too.'

I stood up and said: 'You're new.'

'I know,' Alpha replied impishly, 'I was made just yesterday in a secret factory. The same place they make sarcasm and the dappling of light through trees.'

'I meant to this class.'

'I know what you meant,' she said. 'And I deflected your observation with some sparkling wit. It's called a defence mechanism. I'm enjoying talking to you, and know that as soon as you find out anything more about me, about my family, about my background, then any chance we have of being friends will be gone forever.'

I shook my head. This was weird, but I sort of *liked* her, and I didn't want her to stop talking to me.

'We *are* going to be friends,' I told her. 'In fact, it's too late. It's already happening.'

'You say that now,' Alpha said, 'But when you hear my dark secrets, you'll run a klick. In record-breaking time.'

'I couldn't break a record if I tried,' I said. 'Who wants to talk about family anyway?' I offered her my hand. 'Peter No-Middle-Name Vincent. Officially a friend of Amalfi Del Rey.'

She shook the hand gently, and smiled.

'You'll run a klick,' she said, but warmly.

'A lady of mystery.' I grinned. 'Save the secrets, I don't

even want to know them. How about we just go and get ourselves a drink?'

'Done and done,' Alpha said. 'If you're good, I might even let you pay.'

LinkList/Peter_Vincent

The Dark Secret of Amalfi Del Rey

So, I'll run a klick, huh? But run from what?

Here are my top five guesses:

1. She's a clone

We've been making them for years, because clones without consciousness make perfect transplant banks, but what if she is a clone that accidentally developed a real brain. And escaped from a spare-parts bank? And is on the run?

Likelihood rating: 1/2

2. She's a serial killer

Once upon a time, long, long ago, people were born who were different to everyone else. Instead of going about their lives in the ordinary way, they hid under bridges and jumped out and killed people. OK, so the existence of serial killers is probably a myth, a scary story to tell the kids, but what if she really is one? Better not go under any bridges with her, just to be on the safe side ☺

Likelihood rating: 1

3. She's from a parallel universe

Certain interpretations of quantum theory say that there are zillions of multiple universes, even one where I'm made of cheese and am king of the world. Maybe she's slipped over from the universe next door to borrow a cup of calcium, and she's taking in a few of the sights before she leaves.

Likelihood rating: 1 3/4

4. She's a robot from the future

If you could send a robot back in time, chances are it wouldn't look like a hunk of junk with death rays and stuff, but would be an exact replica of the people it was going to meet in the past. Maybe she is on a mission to change something in her past to avert a global catastrophe, and she's made friends with me because I'm important to her unknowable future-robot scheme.

Likelihood rating: 3

5. She's completely imaginary

Maybe I'm losing my mind and I'm just imagining her. She's like some *alter ego* or something, a figment of my imagination that embodies my essential boredom with the world. And I invented her to make my life a bit more . . . unpredictable.

Likelihood rating: Let's face it, 5

-5-

File: *113/43/00/fgj/Continued*

Source: *LinkData\LinkDiary\Peter_Vincent\Personal*

<LinkDiary Running>

We bought a pair of fruit soys from the refectory and took them outside to sit in the fresh air.

The sun above was scorching hot, but humidity was mercifully low. Yet again the people at Climate Control had managed to pull off another spectacular day, even reassigning the rain to somewhere that actually needed it.

I connected to my jacket with my filaments and in seconds it was a shirt.

Alpha turned a blouse and trousers into a floral-patterned dress.

A rough template, sure, but there were lots of pinks and

yellows in the pattern and it kind of worked.

I really don't usually notice things like that.

We walked past the seats on the terrace and opted for the manicured lawn that sits out the front of the college. There we discovered a mutual liking for mango soy and banana soy, but a mutual dislike for the banango variety.

'Hybrid fruits creep me out,' Alpha announced. 'If you want an apple crossed with a gooseberry – which, in fact, I really *don't* want – then put them in a blender, but don't go combining genes.'

'They'll kick you out of Biogenetics class for statements like that,' I said wryly.

'They'll do that the first time they grade one of my papers,' Alpha said. 'It's my parents that are keen on me getting some science into my life, so here I am, hopping classes in a desperate hunt for something that I'm actually good at.' She frowned. 'Two classes with Ms Donlevy have convinced me that biogenetics is not it.'

'Don't worry,' I said. 'Two lessons aren't enough to make that judgment. You'll find your feet soon.'

'OK, I'll stop talking like the world's number one loser,' she said, and then she looked around us. 'Has everyone here gone study mad?'

'A centrally administered learning-quota adjustment,' I said. 'Or, in everyday linguish, they just raised the bar again.'

'Looks like I picked a great time to arrive,' Alpha said. 'I guess I'll start packing when I get home.'

'No, you had a point today,' I said. 'I just don't think Ms Donlevy is looking to have her thinking changed.'

'But you are.' She arched an eyebrow and it kind of turned her statement into a question.

'I guess so.' I studied the muddy deposits at the bottom of my drink. 'I'm trying to be the perfect student my father wants me to be, but he doesn't seem to notice. Lately, I've been wondering why I work so hard to please him.'

'It's not a bad question,' Alpha said.

'I even signed up for a literature class. My father would freak if he found out.'

Alpha studied my face for a moment, and then shrugged. 'We all have to do things our own way. There's actually no point in following in another's footprints *too* exactly, you'll end up leaving no tracks of your own.'

I nodded.

'The point is that you need to stop worrying about what others think and start concentrating on what *you* want,' Alpha said.

'I guess that's where I hit the wall,' I said. 'I don't know what it is that I want. I just know that this . . .' I gestured around me, 'is not quite it.'

'That's a start, though, isn't it?' Alpha said. 'Sometimes I feel that we all have potential inside us, we just have to discover what our greatness is and how to let it out.'

'I'd settle for quite goodness.' I said.

'The universe has a way of putting us where we need to be, *when* we need to be there,' she said. 'Then it's up to us to rise to the challenge, or turn our back and let someone else be great.' She shook her head. 'You are allowed to tell me to shut up. I mean, the girl most likely to fail school is giving advice on greatness.'

'You won't fail,' I told her. 'You're a lot smarter than you admit.'

'Yeah, I'm sure you won't be saying that when I fail Biogenetics. Spectacularly.'

Before I could stop myself, I heard myself saying: 'I guess I can help you catch up if you need.'

There was a moment's silence that was almost awkward.

'And why, pray tell, would you do that?' Alpha wrinkled her nose.

I gave her an answer that wasn't entirely true. 'I like to help. Especially my friends.'

The misleading bits of that answer were: I only have one true friend, and he has *never* needed my help with his studies before.

But there was something about Alpha that made me think it would be worth helping her out. Because in a few short minutes she had helped *me* out considerably, putting all that stuff into words for me.

'Friends then,' Alpha said. But there was an odd note of sadness in her voice.

'It's the least I can do for my identical fruit soy twin,' I told her.

'You know I *am* going to take you up on your kind offer?'

'Well, let me give you my LinkAddress.' I offered her my hand and she took it in hers. We both turned on our filaments. I gave her my addy, and she blinked to save it, then transmitted hers. I saved it to 'friends', bookmarked it too, and smiled.

'I gotta dash,' I said, standing up. Blades of grass clung to my trousers. I slung my bag over my shoulder. 'I have to spend the afternoon plotting some quantum uncertainties.'

'Hey, have fun with that,' Alpha said.

'I will.' I replied.

Alpha looked as if she was about to say something else, had her mouth open to do it and everything, but then she thought better of it and gave me a smile instead.

Walking back towards the physics block I found myself wondering what had just occurred. I was thinking about the way she was . . . different to anyone else that I had come into contact with.

It was confusing and weird, and I still didn't know why I'd offered to help her out with her coursework, but I suddenly felt like the world had got a little bit lighter, brighter, and a lot more interesting.

<LinkDiary Off>

LinkList/Peter_Vincent

My Top 5 LinkApps

5. Diary Plus+

A filing app for LinkEntries that simplifies the whole tagging process. It could almost be called "Tagging for Dummies". And it supports geotagging, accurate to the metre, of all LinkDiary entries.

Pros: Fast, easy to use, with multiple tags for multiple formats.

Cons: The MemoryFlow view is still seriously laggy, even since the upgrade to Plus+. And the templates are still a little restrictive — couldn't they let us design our own?

Overall: ****

4. BubblePop Evolved

Sometimes you don't want to save the world; sometimes you just want to use your filaments to pop bubbles! For those times, this is the app for you. With multiple levels of difficulty, and a pretty near infinite number of game configurations, this one will just last and last.

But the fun doesn't stop there. There's an add-on that lets you take the app into the real world, harnessing the electrical fields generated by your filaments, and allowing you to physically pop real soap bubbles!

Pros: Frantic and fun.

Cons: Real world implementation is calcium hungry, so stock up on supplements.

Overall: ****

3. CrowdMap

Like FaceSpace, and MyBook, CrowdMap is a social linking programme that brings all your bookmarks and LiveFeeds into one easy-to-manage app.

Pros: Cross-posting between social connection pages.

Cons: Geotagging still a little buggy.

Overall: ****1/2

2. LinkHangers

What can I say? A perfect filing system for all your templates, file by colour, style, material. There's even a place to put your embarrassing CosPlay purchases, but I would keep quiet about that if I was you.

Pros: Simply the best there is.

Cons: None.

Overall: *****

1. Last Quest: Diamond Dust

OK, it's just a shrunk down version of Last Quest, and is a series of smaller campaigns that don't devour huge chunks of your free time, but its vast number of mini-games will keep you busy on slider trips and between lectures.

Pros: Those addictive mini-games.

Cons: The graphics are a lot less convincing than in the full game, but then I think they're pretty cute ☺

Overall: *****

-6-

File: *113/44/00/fgj*

Source: *LinkData\LinkDiary\Peter_Vincent\Personal*

<LinkDiary On>

On the way back from college, the northbound stretch of the city slideway was snarled up around New Lincoln Heights.

Outside the slider's window, a forest of huge, sparkling, milk-white towers rose up from a seedbed of jewel-like structures.

Inside the slider, people were getting agitated.

I reluctantly stopped reading *Gulliver's Travels* on my LinkPad and connected to the Link by thinking *Open Link* and then *News. Local.* The information started to flow into my mind and I narrowed the stream to concentrate on news relevant only to my GPS position.

It was reporting that a crew was clearing another leaper off the tracks.

It was the third one in the city this week.

It'd take a whole lot of time for the authorities to sort out, so I grabbed my college bag from the seat, stuffed my Pad into it and made for the slider doors. I was still a couple of klicks away from Amicus Park, my station, but I started to walk anyway.

I passed a group of onlookers who were trying to see over the medical cordon, to catch a glimpse of the person who had let gravity solve their problems for them.

I shook my head. I have no idea what it is in human nature that makes people want to see sights like that. The world was falling apart and there were people craning their necks to see its final collapse.

I stopped.

Whoa. I thought. *Where did that thought come from?*

I quickly opened a media channel on the Link and shopped for some music to shut my brain up.

All, literally, in the blink of an eye.

I downloaded something with old-fashioned guitars and

a pounding – almost industrial – beat.

I set my stride to the rhythm and tried not to do any more thinking.

Within five minutes I'd reached the foot of the crystal towers I'd been looking at from the comfort of the slider.

New Lincoln Heights rose up into the sky, a crystalline neighbourhood that had literally been grown from minerals seeded into the earth.

Where the sun struck its angled surfaces rainbows were formed, making the buildings seem less than solid.

I slowed then stopped, just to take in the wonder of the sight close up, but I was holding up the flow of the pedestrian walkway and people started grumbling.

The city's planners were growing the Crystal Projects to house the rising number of Strakerites who, it seems, have decided that they need to live separately from the rest of the population.

My father calls the new developments *the diamond ghettoes*, and the Strakerites superstitious primitives. He blames all of society's problems on the Strakerites, as if they are deliberately making his life harder. His opinions are

48

reinforced daily by LinkStreams transmitted by people who already agree with him.

I've started to doubt the wisdom of drawing one's opinions from the same data well every day. But my father refuses to acknowledge that there *is* another way. You either agree with him or you are wrong.

My walk had taken me around New Lincoln Heights and on to the Middle Beltway that served as a dividing line between the ordinary and the Strakerite neighbourhoods. Rush hour restrictions meant that the beltway was reserved for solar gigs and battery carts, but even taking all other vehicles out of the equation there were still four solid lanes in both directions standing at gridlock.

We came down from the trees, built cities over paradise, and suddenly we're all sitting in traffic.

It seemed absurd, as if the more we progressed as a race, the smaller our lives actually became.

Maybe that was why I was turning to English lit. To try to find something larger for my life.

Or maybe it was simply that my mother loved to read.

She had owned a small collection of *real* books; wondrous

old things that smelled of dust and vanilla and almonds and wood. Some of my earliest memories are of her, sitting by the side of my bed, an impossibly old volume held in one hand, while the other turned the pages as she read to me.

Wonderful memories, but they always left me feeling sad and bewildered: tainted forever, I guess, by the fact that she is gone.

My father must have disposed of her books. I remember him disapproving of her reading.

I carried on moving towards home and I thought of Lemuel Gulliver making his way through lands that made no sense. Before long I was smiling.

Strakerite

From Linkipedia, the everywhere encyclopedia

A Strakerite is a believer, practitioner or follower of Strakerism, a movement of people who believe that human beings are, at crucial points in human history, upgraded by alien programmers.

The term derives from the Kyle Straker Tapes, a set of audio cassettes believed to have been recorded by Kyle Straker, a fifteen-year-old boy, in the early years of the 21st century. Much controversy surrounds the tapes themselves and their later transcription, which was published in book form as 0.4.

More>>>>>

-7-

File: *113/44/00/fgj/Continued*

Source: *LinkData\LinkDiary\Peter_Vincent\Personal*

<LinkDiary Running>

I walked and the people of the city flowed around me, lost in their own interior worlds. Faces passing, eyes open, but distant. Most of them were surfing the Link while walking.

The Link, we are told, is our friend.

It allows us to work, chat, swap data, study, shop, play games, watch films, listen to music, connect with friends, take a virtual vacation or augment reality with filters, menus and even animations – the same things we have been doing for thousands of years – on the go. The Link is there in our heads – there's no onboard hardware and the software that runs it is external, carried through the air.

It works, we're reminded, because of our marvellous capacity for filament networking. Yes, we've always been able to swap data through our filaments; the Link just provides a constant connection without the need for physical contact. It's not actually as intense as doing it by filament networking, it is a lot less immersive, and that's why people can be plugged into the Link and go about their daily business.

The Link helps by screening out the unnecessary details of the environment.

Like, well, the environment.

It makes us more productive.

More useful.

I rarely use it for anything but listening to music when I'm out and about. That and keeping my LinkDiary, but that takes no effort, or even conscious thought. LinkDiary just happens when you turn it on. You don't even realise you're making an entry, most of the time.

Like it's second nature. Or habit.

I can't remember a precise moment when I decided to stop using the Link for everything, all the time; I'm not even certain that there *was* a moment where I consciously *chose* to cut down on my use.

It just got so exhausting to have all those voices and images, all that data, in my head the whole time. So I experimented with spending time off-Link, every now and again.

You know, I've been thinking that my life is getting a little weird since I signed up to study literature, but I might as well be honest with myself and say that it actually started some time before that.

There's something about the Link that scares me, that makes me wonder if . . .

?

?

<LinkDiary Crashing>

<Read/Write Error>

1010193498230413091830434709568742653491847192587349579304571394587905237459812375498314759813749128374938547345931440595982349583240569863541=3432345-

9045923=450931=5023049645688=304toireuto2309[4
5irueqklr;thjewrt234po5uwq;eherthwrklthwetu243u59irj;qlek
t34oi43u5[135i3t43mummy41290349560843poi5u35i353

    <LinkDiary Off>

    <Reboot> <New Entry>

    ?Error Report? = <no>

<LinkDiary Resume>

Wow . . . that hurt . . . a headache . . . diary crashed . . . it's never done that before . . . has it?

What the hex was I . . .?

Ah, yes.

Walking.

Home.

Headache.

I used my filaments to increase my endorphin levels and to block the pain. It was a crude job, but I didn't want to use the Link to get a proper painkilling package. I didn't want to use the Link at all, but after a few paces I could no longer remember why that might be.

So I just kept walking.

It's weird but the simple act of walking distances has become alien to us now. My legs started hurting after ten minutes of walking; my knees and my feet starting to protest my decision to leave the comfort – and laziness – of the slider.

'. . . your MEMORIES.' Someone suddenly shouted, and it made me flinch.

I looked around me.

The human river flowed, upstream and down, tuned into the world, but no longer seeing it.

Had I imagined the voice? It seemed disturbingly possible, a lot more likely than one of the Link-tuned crowd suddenly shouting something out.

I was about to carry on walking when the voice tore through the air again.

'MEMORIES!'

Just then the crowd parted a little and I saw who was making the noise.

On a street corner, a man was standing on some kind of

box or crate, shouting at people as they passed him.

'If all that you REMEMBER is all that you are: who are you today? And who were you yesterday?' The man demanded.

But no one was even looking at him; to the passers by it was as if he wasn't even there.

He looked wild, with a long black mane of hair plastered down on top of his skull. His face was lined and creased by age. And his eyes blazed with what I could only describe as madness.

I was staring, but I couldn't help myself. It was such a weird thing to see; to hear.

'YOU!' he roared, and I realised he was pointing at me.

Don't look at him; pretend you haven't seen him, I thought.

There was a scuffling noise, then a thud, and when I looked up again the man had leaped down from his makeshift platform and was standing in front of me, blocking my way. Those mad eyes of his were wide and staring.

Staring at me.

I suddenly remembered an odd poem that my mother used to whisper to me when I was small. Something from a long, long time ago. It used to scare me when I was small. It scared me now, too.

> We must not look at goblin men,
> We must not buy their fruits:
> Who knows upon what soil they fed
> Their hungry thirsty roots?

I shuddered.

If goblin men ever really truly existed, then surely this was one of them.

'They can rub away our memories,' he said as I stood there trying to figure out how to get out of the situation. I angled myself to go past him but he stepped in my path again.

'They can change them into any colour or flavour they like,' he persisted, putting his face close enough to mine that I could feel his breath.

I thought: *humour him*, and nodded, enthusiastically.

'My memories are blue,' I said. 'And butterscotch.'

The man's face went from 'insane' to 'enraged'. It only

took a widening of the eyes and a tightening of the jaw.

'HOLES!' he screamed. 'They dig them in your brain and things fall into them. Things crawl out of them. The answer's under your feet and it always has been, you're just too brainwashed to look. Haven't you seen the symbols? The new . . .'

I was backing away, getting ready to run, when the man's eyes suddenly went blank and his face seemed to sag.

He stood there, almost immobile.

In fact the only sign that he was still capable of movement was his hands, clenching into fists then unclenching, at his sides.

I took my chance and stepped around him, afraid that those hands would suddenly reach out for me, that they would grab me, clenching and unclenching around my throat.

I made it ten metres from him before I realised that I was actually running. Slowing to a walk, I looked back over my shoulder. The man was still there; still motionless; still doing that thing with his hands.

I looked away from him and hurried along the bands of the slideway.

-8-

File: *113/44/00/fgj/Continued*

Source: *LinkData\LinkDiary\Peter_Vincent\Personal*

<LinkDiary Running>

At the end of the long walk: home.

The mad words of the strange man had finally stopped ringing around in my head and I was thinking about Alpha again, trying to work her out.

I'd genuinely never met anyone like her before. She was clever in a way that I wasn't. Not a learned-by-rote-in-a-classroom clever. She saw *through* the surface of things. I liked that.

I stood in front of the house's security fence – a solid wall of energy that surrounds our home – and wondered what it was that we thought we were keeping out. Sure, crime is on the increase for the first time in generations, but you don't actually have to increase 'zero' that much for a bar chart to look like things are getting out of hand.

Perhaps it was part of my father's distrust of Strakerites that made him so cautious; sometimes he referred to them as 'barbarians' and maybe he truly pictured them storming the gates of his castle, wanting to bring the world down into chaos and superstition.

And he *had* been publicly against the idea of teaching Strakerist ideas in schools and colleges.

If the Strakerites were as crazy as my father made out, maybe he was right to be cautious.

My hand disgorged half a dozen filaments, and I watched as the thin, whip-like structures merged with the circuitry in the guard post. The fence unlocked to my physical signature.

Filament biometrics. Got to love them.

The door section of the wall dimmed — but didn't shut off entirely — and I moved into it, feeling the cold, tingling sensation as it performed its final verification checks. If, by some almost impossible chance, an intruder used filament identification to fool the guard post, the full body scan would betray them and hold them inside its containment field until help arrived.

I have no idea who would answer such a call. The idea of a police force is *so* outdated. I guess it would be the employees of a private security company, but I'd never asked.

A paranoid part of my brain wondered if the scan could be configured to read my LinkDiary — or even my thoughts — but I pushed such fears away and just waited until the scan confirmed what I already knew: I was Peter Vincent, and I was allowed through the security fence.

My home is an old-fashioned manor house recreated in liquid granite, and finished in real wood. Not much of it, mind, but enough that it feels supremely decadent. You need a permit for real wood these days, and very few people are granted one.

There are some stables out back, and about two acres of land. It's a far cry from the cramped, chaotic living conditions of the majority of the city's population.

The path leads up from the gates and through an elegant but spartan front garden that had more space than anyone in New Lincoln Heights could ever dream of owning.

Genetically recreated peacocks paraded about the lawns, their electric plumage catching the half-light of a slowly descending twilight. I stopped to watch a neon male fanning out his digital feathers, sending rays of many colours in all directions.

Most people have never even seen a peacock, and we have a half-dozen of them in our garden. Previously that would have given me a real sense of pride; today it just felt wrong somehow. Unjust. It didn't diminish the beauty of the birds, but it sort of tarnished them a little in my mind.

On both sides of me were vast bushes of some hybrid plant with purple, bell-shaped flowers that bobbed in a faint breeze. I could hear the electric drone of a couple of bees at work within them and found myself wondering what real bees had sounded like.

I was halfway up the path when the front door suddenly opened and my father came out. He was dressed in a sharp, metallic suit and the expression on his face told me that he was impatient and angry.

I felt a sudden jolt of panic that my father had found out about my little course change. I mean, it would only have taken a LinkMail from the college to tell him that I had put in the request. Maybe that was the kind of thing they notified parents about, I don't know.

Anyway, I didn't need to worry.

Not about that, anyway.

'You're late,' My father said.

Uh-oh. I thought. *What have I forgotten?*

'I know,' I said defensively. 'They were scraping up another leaper off the tracks of the slideway and I had to walk.'

'Tonight of all nights,' he said, and his tone betrayed the fact that he was still holding me personally responsible for my lateness. 'Hurry up and get changed.'

'Changed?' I asked him.

He looked exasperated.

'You *do* know what tonight is, don't you?' he barked.

I scanned my LinkCalendar and found nothing there to help me. Which meant that it was my father's error, not mine. If he had told me it would have been automatically entered on to the calendar.

Still, it wouldn't help to point out who was to blame. So I just shook my head and tried to look sorry.

My father wasn't impressed. Status report: normal, then.

I can't remember the last time my father was anything but unimpressed with me. Since my mother . . . left . . . he's been increasingly worried about what he calls his *legacy* — the ideas and inventions he'll leave behind when he takes off into the great unknown — and I am, I guess, an important part of that legacy. He wants me to carry on with his work, to take his ideas forward, so that a future historian will look back and say *this is where it all started, and David Vincent was the man who started it.*

But here's the thing.

I'm nothing like him, not really. For my father, work is everything. And life is just something that happens in the gaps *between* the discoveries and the theories.

He'd work twenty-four hours a day, if he could. Fun and poetry and music and . . . I don't know . . . just hanging out . . . are only distractions to him. He's only truly happy when he's saving the world, or building the next great supercomputer, or meeting up with his high-powered friends and planning the future of the human race.

Me, I like the moments in between: I like goofing off and

65

relaxing, kicking back and letting the world pass by me.

I'm not *driven* like my father. I realise that I might have a part to play in society, but it's never going to be the only thing I use to define myself.

My father was looking at me like I was an important experiment that had just failed.

'The Keynote?' he said, as if that was going to be any help to me at all.

I did some more head shaking. Paired it up with a blank look.

'I'm addressing the Science Council,' he explained. 'And their families. A little bit of enforced PR that I was *expecting* you to attend.'

I guess 'expecting' is more real to my father than 'asking'.

I gave him a nod.

'I'll get changed,' I said.

I scanned the Link for something appropriate to the occasion, found a Nevri Bartlett evening suit, which was expensive, but elegant. I paid with FlashCash, downloaded the template, and then let my filaments turn my outfit into the suit.

It took seconds. And fit perfectly.

The material was iridescent, and alternated between midnight blue and a much lighter LED purple depending on the angle that light hit it.

And it had a cleaning function, like a lot of designer attire, which meant I didn't even need to take a shower.

'Ready,' I said. 'Let's go.'

LinkList/Peter_Vincent

My Top 5 Virtual MiniBreak Destinations

5. Old New York

OK, its programming is a little loose and there are far too many recursive glitches for it to be a long stay (an hour and a half is my longest visit) but what it lacks in subtlety it more than makes up for with its sense of danger.

Whether taking a cab ride through Times Square, eating bagels and MacDougal's hamburgers in the famous Restaurant of Liberty, or just walking around Linkin Park after dark, there's a real sense that anything can indeed happen in the red white and blue apple.

4. The Cold Wilds

One of the newer virtual experience packages, the Cold Wilds is a kind of snowboarding environment, but it's a hex of a lot more than that.

The physics have infinite levels of customisation, so you can make a mere half-pipe into a zero-gravity death run; or switch gravity to any surface so that you can grind horizontally along the side-lock courses.

3. Centra-Sphere

After a complete overhaul, the new Centra-Sphere has opened, and it was worth the wait!

VibrAtioN is the new must-visit attraction, a neutral field environment that turns sound into sensory stimulus. You haven't lived until you've felt your LinkTunesLibrary converted into waves that surround your body and physically interact with you. A LinkUpgrade to v2.14 will even allow generation of unique imagery skimmed from your library! Wow.

2. Sea-Side Evolved

Back in the day, the world used to lo-o-o-ove the seaside, but then coastal protection, marine conservation and sand mites made it a thing of the past.

Now it's back in virtual form and, although it is a little weird getting used to doing nothing more than lying in the sun (a UV-neutral version) and picking sand out of everything you own, it's surprisingly relaxing.

1. Last Quest Resort

Big surprise about my number one!

This experience kind of transplants the whole Last Quest world into a vivid – although still a little underdeveloped – interactive experience. Go Chickaboo racing at the Crystal Plains Raceway, or search for treasure in the Vile Wastes; challenge one of the Knights of Fear to a duel, or fly with the MechMages through the skies of Avalon; steal the magic of the Summoners, or just shop at the KingTown Market. It's all there, and the experience is so immersive, so breathtakingly beautiful, that it is my absolute favourite getaway.

Still a little on the pricey side, but perfect to escape from real life.

-9-

File: *113/44/00/fgj/Continued*
Source: *LinkData\LinkDiary\Peter_Vincent\Personal*

<LinkDiary Running>

The Science Council is an architect's layer cake of metal and glass on the southernmost edge of New Cambridge. Surrounded by a lush park, it rises up with a look of unshakeable confidence in its own importance.

As well it might.

It is, after all, where all the *really* clever people research the future, developing the technologies and building the devices that will make the general population's lives easier. And lining their own pockets.

I don't know how I became so cynical. There's no reason for it really. I'd lived a privileged life and I had wanted for nothing — except my mother back, I guess, and that wouldn't happen even if we had all the credit in the world — so there really was no reason for me to think such things.

My father's Mercedes-Royce Electric Shadow is flashed with premium software, so it's allowed to travel on the higher tiers of the beltway. Below us was another gridlock, but up here — on the pay-as-you-drive tiers — there were fewer than twenty cars in both directions between home and the south of the city.

The rolling traffic restrictions put in place to deal with the vast numbers of road users simply don't apply if you have the software, and the money, to roll out on the private beltways.

My father was silent as he steered the car towards our destination. He had stopped speaking pretty much the moment I suited up. I'd tried to get him talking, but he made it clear that he was thinking about his Keynote speech, and preferred not to be distracted by conversation.

Or *my* conversation, anyway.

Which, I guessed, was because of his latest research project. I didn't get to hear much about it; it was classified work for the World Government. I assumed it was an extension of his usual research into the construction of a new way of computing, but, for all he told me, he could have been working on a way to turn the sky into blueberry jam.

I might have pressed him, just to stave off the boredom, but I got an instant message on the Link.

?Are you going to be there tonight? Perry hit me.

/Yeah./ I bounced back. */I'm on a three line whip./*

?What does that even mean? Perry queried.

/I really don't know./ I offered. */Something my mother used to say. She was obsessed with political history, so I guess it's something that's long gone now./*

Perry waited, to give the reference to my mother the proper measure of respect, then came back with: */Whatever./*

?I take it you're attending too? I asked.

/Pops wouldn't take no for an answer./

?Who are you going to be wearing?

?What are you, the fashion police?

/Just want to make sure I'm looking better than you./ I said, only half joking.

/Bound to be. Pops has put a ceiling on my Flash. I'm reusing an old template./

/Tough./

?Ain't it. You?

/Bartlett./

/Oh. Big guns, huh. Well, I submit to your superior might./

/Good to hear that you know when you're beaten. Always give a fellow his due, that's my motto./

?Since when? I asked, incredulously.

/Since now./ Perry replied.

I don't even know what it is about Perry and me and our clothes. It started when we were in prep, and has just kind of continued.

It's like a designer escalation; a clothes war.

Trying to dress the best for events we were both attending.

Looked like tonight I was going to win.

I was about to disconnect when Perry said something weird.

?Hey, did you hear the latest about the ghosts on the Link?

?Huh? I had no idea what he was talking about.

/Oh, Peter./ Perry said. */Sometimes I forget just how little*

you really see of the Link. The ghosts in the photographs.
Everyone's talking about them./

　/Not everyone./ I said. *?So what are we talking?*

　/Ghosts./ Perry reiterated. */Molly Grabowitz saw ghosts,*
and they passed through her photo albums and left an
image of themselves in every photo. Ruined them all. Here's
a bookmark. You can view the photos. Pretty scary stuff./

　?Who the hex is Molly Grabowitz?

　/Oh, boy. Look her up. I gotta go./

　/Catch you there./ I said.

　/Most def. Later./

I smiled.

The Link might be a bank of the world's knowledge,
accessible by anyone with the right credit rating, but it's also
a place where all the world's crazy people meet up and trade
conspiracy theories.

　For some reason Perry seems to find the things the crazy
people leave on the Link, and feels it's his duty to direct me
towards them.

　So he's had me checking out cats the size of horses,
which even a rudimentary grasp of the principles of photo

manipulation should have told him was faked.

I searched for the name he'd given me on Linkipedia and found that Ms Grabowitz was an actress in some new Link Opera.

Probably had a new role coming up and the ghost thing Perry seemed so interested in was just some promotional viral to get the world talking about her.

I didn't even bother to follow Perry's link to the photos.

interlogue

File: *224/09/12fin*

Source: *LinkData\LinkDiary\Live\Peter_Vincent\Personal*

\<RUN\>

This is hard, this next entry.

I'm trying to get everything in the right order, to make sure that the thing I'm committing to permanent memory is indeed the event that occurred and not some altered, corrupted version of the truth.

This next bit, though, has been altered, and I'm not just talking about the way the diary crashes at a crucial part of the proceedings.

There are things missing, I feel it intuitively, but I have no way of filling in the gaps, of physically remembering the event so that I can reconstruct it from memory.

That's the thing about the Link, you see, the thing that we never thought about or acknowledged, or even suspected: We have stopped remembering things. We trust the Link to remember them for us.

The problem is we shouldn't have trusted the Link to remember things the way they happened. Details can be changed, and memories edited.

History itself can be rewritten. You only need to change a word here, an event there. Even things like emphasis and importance can be up or downgraded to make history say what they want it to say. To make it read how they want it to read.

My memories are no different. I remember things because I put them on the Link. That's what we all do.

But I can no longer be sure that what's stored there is the truth.

-10-

File: *113/44/00/fgj/Continued*

Source: *LinkData\LinkDiary\Peter_Vincent\Personal*

<LinkDiary Running>

At the doors of the Science Council my father gave me a tired-looking smile, told me to find a seat in the chamber, and disappeared into the crowd milling around the foyer. I stood there for a few seconds feeling abandoned, then shrugged myself out of it.

I made my way down a couple of white corridors and then through an arch that led into the Council's main chamber.

My father once told me that the chamber was modelled after a natural cave formation that had been discovered somewhere in South America. Now, walking into it, I was struck by the weirdness of its design. It had a ceiling that stretched high over the heads of the assembled people, with sculpted stalactites dangling down. Some of the stalactites were two metres long, and made of a material that made them look as if they were natural formations, made over many thousands of years.

Except for the fact that they were hanging from the ceiling of a room in a modern building.

Still, it sort of took your breath away just being in the room and I realised that – as a percentage – very few people got the opportunity to see it for themselves.

I looked around for Perry, but couldn't see him, so I flashed him an enquiry and he replied with an image of the inside of the chamber, then an image of his seat number: Row F, Seat 23.

I made my way towards him.

Seating was in tiered concentric semicircles, facing a central hub, and I found Perry easily.

'Looking sharp,' Perry greeted.

I nodded at his suit, a dark plum-coloured Nehru affair with a cravat that changed colour every twenty-or-so seconds. It might have been a suit I'd seen him wear a couple of times before, but the chromatic cravat was something new and, I had to admit, a pretty neat touch.

'Not looking so bad yourself,' I told him, taking the seat next to him. 'What have I missed?'

Perry rolled his eyes.

'A talk on the place of science in our brave new world, complete with a holographic presentation that was inferior to the ones we were doing for show-and-tell to the class in pre-prep.' Perry faked a yawn. 'Look, we're nearly sixteen years old, have we really got nothing better to be doing of an evening?'

'Are we not our fathers' sons?' I replied, then added: 'They didn't have the holographic giraffe again, did they?'

'And the duck-billed platypus,' Perry said scornfully. 'But they'd re-skinned them both in company colours, with a logo and everything.'

'*Making nature better, one animal at a time*,' I said. 'I'm *sooo* sad I missed that.'

'I just bet you are,' Perry replied. 'Told your father about the course change yet?'

'Of course,' I said, waited a couple of beats and finished it with: 'Not.'

Perry's cravat switched from orange to grey.

'Leave it long enough and you'll have graduated by the time he finds out,' he smirked.

'That's kind of what I'm hoping,' I said.

Perry suddenly looked around in a decidedly shifty way, and lowered his voice into a conspiratorial whisper. 'So what's this I've been hearing about you and a mystery girlfriend?'

I swallowed and it must have been loud enough for Perry to hear.

'I beg your pardon?' I said, in my best version of a 'deny everything' voice.

Perry just grinned.

'You can't hide your filthy little secrets from me,' he said. 'There were confirmed reports, from many sources, of a secret tryst between my main man Peter and an as-yet-unidentified female. I just want to hear your side of it so I can keep spreading the rumours.'

I shook my head. My cheeks felt hot. I'd kind of thought

that lunch with Alpha wouldn't have been important enough for anyone to even notice, let alone remark upon.

'Nothing to tell,' I muttered. 'I did buy a girl a fruit soy, but the last time I checked that wasn't really an important occurrence.'

Perry tutted.

'What?' I asked.

'OK,' Perry said. 'Since when is fraternising with girls anything other than an important occurrence?'

'Well...'

'The answer, my friend, is: *never*.' Perry raised his eyes to the ceiling, then back down.

'It was a soy,' I said feebly. 'Sometimes a soy is just a soy.'

'Matter. Of. Opinion,' Perry shot back, making three sentences out of one. 'Now quit dodging the question and spill the goods.'

But I really didn't want to *spill*.

I wanted Perry to shut up.

He knows as well as I do that I'm not supposed to befriend girls, not yet. I am practically *forbidden* from having any female friends, let alone a *girlfriend*.

Romantic love is something that is scheduled in when I hit twenty-one.

It's standard practice that when I make that age, a list of suitable candidates will be drawn up for me, and I will have a month to decide which three are going to make it on to my shortlist.

Negotiations will begin, final criteria will be set, and a month after that I'll be announcing my engagement.

If my father found out about me sharing a fruit soy with *a girl*, then it would be even worse than him finding out about me swapping to a 'soft' course like English Literature.

The latter could be viewed as an error of judgement, a slip, a moment of madness.

The former would be viewed as something else entirely.

Disobedience.

I guess that was why I was so worried to hear that I was already the subject of college gossip. In a world where all information flows around the Link, nothing is private and no one can tell where it will end up.

My mother used to quote someone called Horace when she came across Link gossip. She'd say: *a word once let out of its cage cannot be whistled back again,* and I had never really thought about what it meant.

Now I knew.

People talked and stories spread. It made me feel angry.

I was saved from these dark thoughts, however, by the bell. Or, rather, by the start of the Keynote address.

My father walked out into the speaking area and the hubbub of voices around us fell into a respectful silence. I opened my mouth, as if I was just going to tell Perry the details he wanted, then closed it and shrugged.

He rolled his eyes at me and mouthed: 'Later.'

I turned away and watched my father getting ready to speak.

He looked calm, relaxed even, which is something I'm not really used to seeing in him. For my father, I'm sure, anxiety is the fuel that drives him. That and anger.

As he checked his LinkPad for the playback for his presentation I even think I saw him smile.

Suddenly the room went into darkness.

Total darkness.

There were a few whispers around us, and someone coughed.

Then my father's voice said: 'Imagine this. The moment before the universe sprang into being. Nothingness. Void. Blackness. Emptiness. It was a special kind of nothing that we can't even begin to describe. Because, I'm afraid, we weren't there. No one was. *Nothing* was.' He paused. 'Then: it happened.'

Suddenly a tiny dot appeared, holographically, in the middle of the darkness, and the contrast made it seem painfully bright.

'A billionth of a second into the Big Bang, this tiny bubble was formed.' My father's face was illuminated on one side by the light. He looked a bit sinister, if I'm honest. 'It was a fraction of the size of a single atom, yet it contained everything our universe is, everything it would become.'

The bubble started swelling outward, and coloured dots accelerated outward from within it. Red ones and yellow ones, brown ones and black.

'Everything in the universe,' he continued, 'was packed into something that small: every atom in the universe, the seeds of planets and stars. Some people find that utterly amazing. Others find it terrifying. But do you know what I say to myself every time I consider the Big Bang?'

The image changed, suddenly, to a view of the planet Earth, seen from space, then quickly zoomed out to show our solar system; then the galaxy that we are but a tiny part of; and finally thousands of galaxies sitting in coal black space.

'I think: *all that information, in something so small*, I want to make *one of those*.'

The image of the universe faded out and the chamber's lights gradually came back on.

My father looked around at the faces staring at him and smiled.

'OK, that's just me, I guess,' he said. 'But we do have a serious problem.'

A beautiful hologram of the Earth, spinning in space, appeared in front of us.

'This world of ours is awash with information that needs both processing and storage.'

An image showing coloured lines representing that information appeared around the Earth. It didn't take long before the Earth itself was obscured by all that information.

'Our Smart Cities are built around huge computer networks that control everything from lighting to heating to the environment. Our medical computers are so very sophisticated that they require vast resources just to manage the systems that keep us healthy.

'Then there's the Link. It is the most complex computer network ever created, managing billions of pieces of information every second, and each entry made in a LinkDiary carries not just text, but pictures, sound files and video.

'We are reaching a point where the demand for space for our physical data is overtaking our supply. We are being saturated with data, and we are reaching the limits of the Link's capacity.' My father pressed a stud on his Pad and a large display appeared in the air, something that looked like a read out from a heart monitor – a line that blipped upwards and downwards from a central line, creating a jagged pattern of mountains and valleys.

'Example,' he said. 'This jagged line. It's a measurement, in real time, of this room, now. Each peak and trough is simply a graphical representation of the Link activity in this room.

'It's telling us that there are more than 4,000 pieces of data of a size over one terabyte being transmitted to and from this room. That's a *whole* lot of data. And most of you aren't even trying.

'I'd like to suggest that we engage in a small experiment. On the count of three I want everyone in this room to open up the Link and browse to one of your closest bookmarked channels. It doesn't matter which one, but I want everyone to do it. OK?'

He looked around for confirmation, saw it in a few nods and some grunted words of agreement.

'One. Two. Three. *Open Link.*'

I did as I was instructed, opening up a GameServer and navigating my way to a multiplayer fantasy game I've been dipping in and out of. Yeah, I know, GameServers are a waste of time and credits, but I sometimes need to escape from everything by pretending to be a hero in a virtual world. I don't know what that says about me, and I don't particularly care.

The response from the Link was a little sluggish —

everyone else was opening up their own channel — but I still completed the action within a couple of seconds.

The 'Welcome' image from Last Quest XXII greeted me with a *?resume game?* query.

My father's voice cut in.

'And now if everyone could leave the Link open, and bring your attention back to our graphic here . . .'

Looking back at it, I saw the jagged line was now zigging and zagging wildly, with massive peaks and lows and no visible central line.

My father pointed at it.

'Here's the Link when it's busy,' he said. 'You can see quite plainly that data activity is now at incredible levels. From nearly 10,000 to 300,000 TB just by everyone in this room opening a single bookmark. You all probably experienced a slowdown in efficiency. It should illustrate my point: the Link uses enormous amounts of data to operate, and we are running out of the capacity to deal with all this demand.'

My father put his hand into the graphic and pulled at it with his hand. The view of the peaks and troughs suddenly became an image of each individual Link transmission, hundreds of coloured lines in a web-like structure. He teased free a couple of strands and then expanded them.

'Here we are,' he said. 'Someone's been making holiday plans.'

A ShopFront portal for a travel agency hung in the air.

'An adventure holiday. With virtual tours built into the LinkData, all hot-linked to wikis and information databases, with geographical, climatic and historical data. There are multiple links to reviews and photo galleries; and to videos of people who have already been on the holiday.

'One portal, but it contains a massive amount of information; information that has to *exist physically* as stored data. One portal out of billions.'

He screwed the ShopFront up in his hand and stretched it back into a thread. Then he opened up the second thread.

'Ah, I think my son is in the room,' he said, exposing my GameServer page to everyone in the room. A muscled warrior stood in a verdant landscape, a biomechanical sword in his hand.

'A simulated world in which millions of Linked players

can live out digital dreams of chivalry and heroism in a world of magic and adventure.'

I realised that the odds of my father finding my page were too vast for it to be accidental. He had pulled out that thread from the web deliberately, knowing already that it was mine. I felt sick and embarrassed.

It wasn't right that my father was using MY personal data as an example. It was an invasion of privacy, just like showing someone's holiday plans had been.

Perry was grinning again and I felt like reminding him that he and I met up in Last Quest just about every day.

'We'll leave debates about the necessity of such diversions for another time,' he said, and I knew that he was actually talking straight at me. 'What I would like you all to think about is the enormous amount of information required to keep a simulated world like this going.'

He put his fingers into the image and drew out another skein of data strands.

'My son has spent . . .' he expanded one of the strands, 'well over a hundred hours in this one game. In that time he has slain over sixty foes, and completed thirty-nine per cent of the major campaign for the game, as well as working on four non-essential side missions. He has reached Level 45 as a warrior, has died twice and, due to some of his early decisions in the game, is now incapable of gathering two of the best weapons in the game. Shame.'

He winked at the audience and it got a laugh. I felt like they were laughing at me personally. I gritted my teeth and tried to pretend that it was all hilariously funny.

'It seems that there is a LinkPortal for everything,' my father said, shrinking the game back into an anonymous strand amidst hundreds. 'And that, people, is the problem in a nutshell.'

He swatted the strands away and they glistened in the air before disappearing completely.

'Which is why we have been working on new storage methods, and new ways of handling data. It's been a daunting task, but we are just about to reveal the fruits of our labours.'

He paused and looked into the audience.

Then he made a dramatic gesture with his hands and a new image appeared before us.

It took a while to even *begin* to figure out what it was.

It appeared to be a landscape made up of odd, intricate pink trees

It looked like bacteria magnified by the lenses of a powerful microscope.

Or was it a depiction of a coral reef?

I squinted and turned my head to one side, but still had no idea what I was looking at. I did notice, however, that it was moving. The trees, or coral, or whatever the hex they were, swayed slightly from side to side as if moved by a gentle breeze.

'This is what we are calling a "neural forest",' My father explained. 'And it is the very first of its kind. It is, in effect, the answer to all our data needs. It can store and process massive amounts of data, and it requires only one thing in return.'

He looked around, a serious expression on his face. I suddenly realised that he was nervous. I wondered what it was that he had to feel nervous about — if what he said was true, then he had solved one of the pressing issues of our society.

Then he spoke, and I felt nervous too.

'It requires food,' he said, and the whole chamber became

full of very loud voices that @*)(34jiojKH(*{)EWQ*{()Q*RW{)

EQR)(E{)R(ETRE[YTREYERTO9YQR9WQRWEORT9EROY

<STRING>40359345=91ASDKFJASD;GKFKJ)(**65443

<LinkDiary Crashing>
<Read/Write Error>
<LinkDiary Off>
<Reboot> <New Entry>
?Error Report? = <no>

-11-

File: *113/45/02/pdu*

Source: *LinkData\LinkDiary\Peter_Vincent\Personal*

<LinkDiary Resume>

We were on the journey back home, and my father was gripping the steering wheel so hard his knuckles were white.

'Idiots,' he muttered, through clenched teeth. 'Primitive, backwards-looking idiots.'

'You *did* just tell them you've grown a massive human brain in a laboratory,' I said. 'And that, in exchange for food, it will think us out of our problems. You can see why they reacted a *bit* negatively, can't you?'

My father shook his head.

'It's not a *human* brain,' he said, curtly. 'It's artificial. I *made* it.'

'All those people heard was that you had made a brain and you were feeding it. You can understand their reservations . . .'

'No,' my father said sternly. 'I *really* can't.' He connected to the dashboard with his right-hand filaments and the car went on to AutoDrive.

'Do you know how bad things are?' he asked, looking directly at me. His face was deadly serious and his eyes burned like coals in his sockets. 'I mean, *really*?'

I shook my head.

'No,' he said. 'You don't. Nobody does. Because no one has been allowed to see the truth. No matter what people say, the truth really won't set people free, and it's not going to lead them to make a reasoned judgement. The truth will send them screaming into their homes.'

'I can see that we're using a lot of memory . . .' I said.

My father let out a tiny fragment of a laugh that sounded more like a bark than an expression of humour.

'Memory,' he said. 'If only people could see how much of a curse that word has become . . .'

He slammed his left hand on to the dashboard.

I didn't get another word out of him for the rest of the journey, but sitting there in the passenger seat I suddenly realised that there was something different about him.

It was an odd, inexplicable thing. When my father had looked at me so intently, I could have sworn that his eyes were brown.

Dark, hazel brown.

My father's eyes are, and have always been, blue.

<LinkDiary Off>

LinkList/Peter_Vincent

My Top 5 Virtual GameServer Games

5. Everyone's Polo

There's Polo, then there's Everyone's Polo.

With 30 different genetically engineered horses and another 30 cybernetically enhanced battle steeds, you must rise to the top of the pile in the Premier League of Polo, while managing your stables and budgets, and compete against riders with uncanny AI.

It's the next best thing to playing.

4. Dimensiongate 4

The first three Dimensiongate games have tried to fuse puzzle solving, theoretical physics and simple yet effective graphics, but with this one LUminOUS games have really pulled out all the stops. You're still solving complex puzzles based on the laws of physics but it's never looked better, or felt more important, to solve equations.

3. Corona

This one's more than a little controversial: the developers got a lot of bad LinkMins for making what is, in effect, a war simulation. OK, they manage to dress it up in hi-tech, outer-space disguise, but at heart this is all about the pure exhilaration of armed combat. As part of a team of space soldiers, the future of the human race lies in your hands. As does a veritable arsenal of flesh-ripping weaponry.

2. Darkness Eternal

Not my usual kind of fare, but Darkness Eternal is a remarkably gripping and complex thriller that psychologically profiles you as you play, bending the game to fit that profile. It draws its imagery from your own mind, and uses the player's own thoughts against their game character as weapons.

And the coolest thing? If your mood is different, the game is different.

1. Last Quest XXII

As a Warrior of Light, you are tasked with saving the world from falling into chaos at the hands of the cruel tyrant Malevola.

Sounds simplistic?

It isn't.

Last Quest is always at the bleeding edge of game development, and XXII pushes the envelope wide open. Intuitive control systems and filament feedback make this the biggest and best yet.

And the plot – wow, almost totally impenetrable.

You are Cantone, the last in a long line of Warriors of Light and your quest begins as peace reigns, for the first time ever, over the world of Evaline. The Great Machine – a device that cancels out magical energy, has finally removed magic from the planet. It means that, for the first time in its history, Evaline is free of the influences of gods and wizards. Humankind is finally free to make its own destiny.

Only one source of magical power remains – the MotherStone.

Your last task as a Warrior of Light, before retirement to the Hall of Heroes, is to transport the MotherStone from Nimbus, the cloud city, to Eurazia, the site of the great machine, where it can be processed and made safe.

But dark forces led by Malevola, the deathless mage, are determined that your quest should fail. If the MotherStone falls into Malevola's hands before it is made safe then it will become a weapon of unimaginable power – the last magic in a world now defenceless against magic.

-12-

File: *113/45/03/ait*

Source: *LinkData\LinkDiary\Peter_Vincent\Personal*

<LinkDiary On>

Perry flashed me when I got back to my room.

?What the hex was all that about? He wanted to know.

/You were there./ I told him. */You know as much as I do./*

?Yeah, but brains in jars that we're going to start using as computers? Perry said. *?I mean, isn't that all a little too weird, even for your dad?*

It's what I'd been thinking myself, but hearing Perry saying it just made me feel cross and defensive.

/It's hardly brains in jars./ I snapped. *?You were listening, weren't you?*

/I was sitting next to you./ ?Remember?

/I also remember my father saying that the neural forest was an artificially created substance, not a stupid brain in a jar. And your father is working on this thing too./ ?If you're that outraged, why don't you speak to him?

/Not outraged. Just confused./

/It wasn't the most predictable end to a lecture for families . . ./ I said.

?Have you seen a write-up for the Keynote on the Link yet? Perry asked.

/No./ I said.

/Me either./ Perry said. /I was expecting to find reports and outraged threads, but there's nothing./

/That's weird . . . /

/I know, but no one is talking about it. Negative on the chatter front. If I was a paranoid type I might be thinking 'cover up'./

I didn't mention that Perry was one of the most paranoid people I knew.

/Anyway./ he said, /I've got to go, I'm low on calcium. Catch you tomorrow./

/Tomorrow, mate./ I said, and signed off.

Perry's call had left me feeling a weird mixture of things, none of them pleasant. I tried to remember exactly what my father had said in the Science Council chamber, but it was fading in my memory already, as if it had only glanced against the surface of my mind.

I consulted the LinkDiary entries I'd been making live, but some of the data was corrupted and I couldn't access the file.

All the other files before and after it were fine.

My recollections of the Keynote ended with my father saying that his neural forest technology required food. Then there were blocks of scrambled data. When my memory resumed I was already in the car on the way home.

Which was really, really strange.

And, I have to say, kind of worrying.

Timestamps on both memories said there was a thirty-three minute gap between them.

Had I blacked out?

For half an hour?

I wondered if everyone in the room had experienced the missing time.

I flashed Perry back but he wasn't answering so I checked the Link for other people's recollections, but it was just as Perry had said: there wasn't a single mention of the talk anywhere on the whole worldwide network.

It simply made no sense. I mean, a kitten can't wake up without forty different angles of the event turning up on the Link within a minute, so an announcement like my father's, which had shocked even me, how could that not be there?

I was going to investigate further when I felt a tingle on the Link.

From a recent bookmark.

Amalfi.

I think I took two seconds to compose myself before I accepted the feed.

/Hi, Soy Twin./ Alpha's thoughts travelled into mine.

/Hey!/ I thought back. */Good to hear from you./*

/That's what happens when you hand out your addy to just about anyone. They call./

/I'm glad you did./

/I'd put that 'glad' on hold until you hear why I'm calling./

/Don't care./ I said. */Glad still applies./*

?So, what are you up to? Even though it was just Alpha's thoughts over the Link I could tell that she was nervous.

/Don't ask./ I thought.

?That bad, huh? Alpha replied.

/Bad enough./ ?Need some help with college work?

There was a long pause and I thought the Link had glitched out.

Then Alpha came back with: */I — I'm in trouble. I need your help, Peter./*

/Of course. Anything./ ?What can I do?

/I couldn't think of anyone else I could turn to. I need you to . . ./ Alpha broke off, and again there was a pause. *?Can you come and meet me?*

?When?

/Well, I was kind of hoping you could come now./

I smiled.

/Tell me where./ I said. */I'll be right there./*

-13-

File: *113/45/03/ait/Continued*

Source: *LinkData\LinkDiary\Peter_Vincent\Personal*

<LinkDiary Running>

We arranged to meet up in town in half an hour. It was almost eight-thirty already, and the curfew for my age range was eleven-thirty. I needed to get into town, help Alpha with her problem and get back home in a little over three hours.

Tricky enough; and I still had to get out of the house.

I thought about doing something crazy like climbing out my bedroom window, but in the end I decided I'd do it in a more conventional fashion.

I made my way to the front door.

Of course it's not the first time I have gone out at night – Perry and I sometimes meet up, just to hang out – but

108

this felt very different to those occasions.

With every step I expected to hear my father's voice asking me where I thought I was going at this time of night, but I didn't see or hear him even as I was opening the front door.

The night was sticky and warm as I closed the door behind me. I felt a crazy thrill of excitement as I made my way to the security fence.

Amalfi was in trouble.

She asked for my help.

No one has ever asked me for help before.

The fence let me through without any biometric testing. It's really not necessary to screen people coming *out*. If they got in, they are authorised to leave too.

I started towards the slider station, my mind a chaotic blur.

At night the city changes.

The buildings, after storing solar energy all day, release light from every surface and glow in a multitude of different colours, although just *which* colours they are is determined by the person looking at them.

Colour is, after all, an illusion: more to do with how light is decoded after it is received into the eye than an actual, existing property. By switching the way we decode light, we are able – these days – to alter the colour scheme of the world around us. It takes just a thought, and suddenly the city is coordinated to our mood, or personal taste.

I went for 'NeonGlow' and the world lit up in the strong, vibrant colours that are used in Last Quest; a custom filter that I bought just so that I could feel like I was a warrior in an urban fantasy game.

Tragic, isn't it?

But maybe, just maybe, I wanted to be the hero in my own life story for once.

It took me five minutes to get to the slider station and, according to the station's display, it was going to be another fifteen before a slider showed up.

A couple of small groups of people were waiting too. I'm not paranoid like Perry, but I was sure they were staring at me. Which was ridiculous, but I couldn't shake the feeling. I took myself away a little from them on the platform, listening to music and trying not to meet their eyes.

Something interrupted the music, something nagging

me on the Link. I checked it, just to distract myself, I guess.

It was Perry's ghosts-of-the-Link thing from earlier, re-announcing itself.

I thought: *what the hex*, and opened up the Link.

I expected to be underwhelmed.

I was wrong.

-14-

File: *113/45/11/qct*

Source: *LinkData\gallery\shared\Molly_Grabowitz\Images*

<Compare images>

Image_4e7f9backup.jpg <Original>

A woman is standing in front of the Trevi fountain in Rome. The sponsors' logos have been carefully integrated into the fountain's design.

Tall and blonde-haired, the woman seems tiny in front of the complex sculpture of rock, marble and cement that has stood since the 18th century.

Other tourists throng around her, with some of them throwing credit chips into the waters as per tradition. The photo is a fraction overexposed.

Image_4e7f9backup.jpg <Corrupted Element>

The photo is the same as the original with one striking addition.

A young girl is washing her hair in the waters of the fountain behind the woman. She is only half visible, and zooming in on the image only serves to make her less visible. She is partly transparent and you can see the background through her body.

Transparency aside, there is something odd about her, but it's hard to say just what it is. She looks old somehow, but not age-wise. It's almost as if she is from another time period.

Image_14a03f9backup.jpg <Original>

A spectacular view over New London's skyline. Geotagging identifies it as taken from the main observation deck of the TeleLink Tower.

The city spreads out, with the plasteel dome of

Parliament House visible in the background.

The sky is threaded through with the reddish-orange of a summer twilight.

Image_14a03f9backup.jpg <Corrupted Element>

In the foreground, two figures — again transparent — can be plainly seen. A young couple are looking out over the city, and again it is possible to see the photo's background through their bodies.

Their clothing is odd, old-fashioned.

Image_20a13pvbackup.jpg <Original>

A wedding photo of a bride and groom grinning at the camera. The bride is in an exquisite dress, in the traditional bridal colour: light blue.

The pair are standing outside a building, and their expressions are a mixture of happiness and pride.

They are the only people in the photo.

Image_20a13pvbackup.jpg <Corrupted Element>

The couple are not alone in the photograph. A young man can clearly be seen off to the right of the groom. The young man is staring directly into the camera, and it looks like he was in the middle of saying something when the camera caught him. Like the other ghost images, it looks like he is from another period of human history. He is holding his hand up and is showing four fingers.

-15-

File: *113/45/03/ait/Continued*

Source: *LinkData\LinkDiary\Peter_Vincent\Personal*

<LinkDiary Running>

I don't believe in ghosts.

Just like I don't believe in tribal god figures. Or fairies.

If you want an answer to a question about how something in the universe works then you need to answer it with science. In the entire history of the world the answer to a question about the way things work has never been 'magic', 'the supernatural' or 'pixies'.

Examples:

1) An apple falls. *Was it pulled down by hands of angels?* No, I think you'll find the answer to that one is 'gravity'.

2) Bright fire fizzes across the night sky. *Are the Gods*

fighting? No, that one is an electrical discharge, and we have called it 'lightning'.

3) The sun is devoured by blackness in the sky. *Surely the Gods are angry with us?* Uh, no, the moon has just moved in front of the sun. We call that 'an eclipse'.

We learned in pre-prep to look beyond superstition when trying to explain things around us, and to fall back on to the certainties of science.

But looking at those photographs gave me a chill.

Now, I am thoroughly aware that photographs can be manipulated. I have seen pictures of my friends standing on the surface of the moon, and I have seen photographic evidence of the existence of dragons.

I'm friends with Perry, so I've seen more than my fair share of Link hoaxes.

But these photographs were different.

They felt like a sudden window into another, parallel path of existence. They made me think that somewhere, close to us but hidden by some trick of our senses, there was another world, where different people carried on living different lives as we bustled by, unaware of their presence.

Ghosts in the machine, I thought. *I wonder: can they see us?*

The young man in the wedding photo certainly seemed aware that a picture was being taken, looking directly into the camera and holding up those four fingers as . . . *as what?*

I checked the datestamp on the wedding photo.

It was taken three days ago.

The slider arrived and I flashed cash to the ticket machine, taking a seat at the back.

Three days ago, I kept thinking. *Four fingers.*

I used Face-Recognition to scan through the rest of Ms Grabowski's ghosted photographs, using the young man's face as my comparison.

I guess it was a long shot, but sometimes they work out.

I found one more image with the young man in it.

Two women walking down a neon-lit street. The young man in the foreground, looking as out of place and out of time as before.

He was holding up three fingers.

The photo was dated two days ago.

It made me think: *He's counting down!* First four days, then three.

Three days to go: two days ago.

Is he telling us that something is going to happen . . . *tomorrow?*

-16-

File: *113/47/04/cbt*

Source: *LinkData\LinkDiary\Peter_Vincent\Personal*

<LinkDiary Running>

I got into town, only to find that Alpha was already there, waiting for me.

The cube-shaped retail units of downtown were on browse mode. You could still shop if you wanted to, but the service was automated and you couldn't physically see or touch the things for sale until you had paid for them.

Although that was the way most people shopped these days.

You found things on the Link, you paid for them on the Link, and they arrived soon afterwards. I buy clothes on the Link and download their templates, and if I don't like the garment then I don't return it, I just delete it from my virtual wardrobe.

Sometimes the shops seemed like a determined effort to hang on to a past way of living that was almost wholly redundant now.

I guess the past holds a power over us that none of us can quite understand.

Alpha was just where she said she would be. I could tell, even from a distance, that something was troubling her. She was pacing back and forth, her face turned down to the slidewalk, and her shoulders were slumped.

Charles Darwin, captured forever in a liquid granite sculpture, looked down from on high, offering her no advice.

I sped up and called out. Her face brightened when she looked up and saw me approaching.

'Peter,' she said, almost breathless with relief. 'Thank you for coming.'

'I can't resist a damsel in distress,' I said. I think I've already mentioned I didn't talk to many girls, haven't I?

We both pretended I hadn't said the 'damsel in distress' thing, found a bench and sat down.

'Nice threads,' she said, and I realised that I was still wearing the Bartlett suit.

'Yeah, sorry, I should have dressed up,' I joked lamely.

Alpha's face was tense and pale, even in the light of the glowing buildings. It made me remove the stupid filter and see her in the natural glow of stored sunlight.

'What's happened?' I asked.

Alpha shook her head.

I didn't know whether that meant she didn't know, or she wasn't ready to say just yet, so we sat there in silence and looked across at the lights of the city.

I've seen pictures of Cambridge as it was hundreds of years ago – there are thousands of them in the library at the college – and it's always hard to match up that city of the past with the present one. New Cambridge was now little more than a clone of every other city on the planet, with the same kind of buildings and the same branded retail units.

'I looked you up,' Alpha said finally. 'I mean, a profile and all that. I didn't find out much about you, but I thought I could trust you.'

'You can.'

'Yeah, well, I don't trust people all that easily.' Alpha's face was half in shadow, half brightly lit and it reminded me of my father's face, sometime recently, but I couldn't for the life of me remember where or when.

Alpha sat there for a moment, looking like she was thinking something through, then she puffed her cheeks out and suddenly blurted: 'Look, my family are Strakerites. Feel free to run away screaming. I won't hold it against you.'

I tried to dismiss her fears with a laugh. 'And there was me thinking your big secret was that you were a serial killer.'

Alpha looked shocked.

'I would have thought being a Strakerite was worse,' she replied.

I shook my head.

'But your . . . your father . . .?' she began.

'My father may think that Strakerites are dangerously deluded, but then he *is* the man who killed off the last of the Earth's bees.' I reached out and touched the back of Alpha's hand, gently, with my fingertips. 'Me, I think everybody is entitled to their own opinions on things.'

Alpha looked at me, her eyes squeezed into suspicious

slits, like she was still expecting me to run away, or insult her or something. What she saw must have surprised her because her face softened, and her eyes opened wide.

'You're different,' she said, quietly.

'I am? To what?'

'To everyone else,' Alpha said. 'I told you that I was in trouble,' she said, 'but that wasn't the complete truth. It's not me, exactly, it's my dad.'

'Why, what's wrong with him?'

'That's the problem,' Alpha said, close to tears. 'I don't know. He's . . . gone.'

'Gone?'

'Disappeared. No one's seen him. He was supposed to meet my mother for lunch today and didn't turn up. She couldn't reach him in the Link. She checked everyone she could think of and no one has seen him since he left the house this morning.' She grimaced. 'Yes, we live in New Lincoln Heights.'

'Looks like an amazing place,' I said. 'I like the crystal engineering methods – the buildings look like diamonds or something.'

'It's a scary place.' Alpha said. 'It may look great on the outside, but the way the authorities are cramming Strakerites in . . . it's becoming a slum.'

I thought about what my father said about them being ghettoes, and it was odd to be hearing the same sort of ideas being spoken by someone on the *other side* of those crystal walls.

'So where do you think he's gone?' I asked her. 'Your father, I mean.'

She shrugged.

'If he was the only one that has disappeared I guess I wouldn't be worried,' she told me. 'But I have to show you something. I just don't want you to freak out on me.'

'I'll try not to,' I said, wondering what she was talking about.

She put her hand next to mine and deployed a single filament, and I did the same. We interfaced and she sent an image that hung in the air between us.

The image was a photograph of a row of five people – all men – standing in a line.

They looked like friends, and they were all grinning at the

camera lens, arms around each other's shoulders.

They were all wearing identical lab coats.

I didn't know who four of them were, but was shocked to see that the one in the middle was my father.

He was a fair bit younger-looking, but it was unmistakably him.

Alpha used her hand to point to the people in the photo, starting on the left and working right.

'This is Edgar Nelson,' she said pointing to a tall, thin man. 'His family reported him missing five days ago.'

She moved on to the next, a shorter, grey-haired older man with a kind smile. 'Leonard DeLancey: missing now for three weeks.

'I'm sure you know the next person in the line, and the next one along from your father is *my* dad, Iain Del Rey. And this man . . .' she pointed to the last in line, an intense-looking man with piercing dark eyes, 'was called Tom Greatorex. Apparently he told his family he was sure he was being followed, and when they didn't believe him he said they were 'in on it too'. They thought he was paranoid, and he ended up jumping from a high building.'

I felt my skin bristle.

'When did that happen?' I asked her, little more than a croak.

'Earlier today,' she said.

I shook my head to clear the image of the bystanders gathering around the person on the tracks of the slideway earlier.

'It seems that our fathers used to work together,' Alpha said. 'And judging by this picture they used to be friends.'

'But if all the others are . . .'

'. . . either missing or dead,' Alpha finished my sentence, 'it means *your father*, the great David Vincent, is probably next on the list.'

-17-

File: *113/47/04/cbt/Continued*

Source: *LinkData\LinkDiary\Peter_Vincent\Personal*

<LinkDiary Running>

It didn't make sense.

Any of it.

So many things were happening today, it was like time was being compressed, and I wasn't fast enough to keep pace.

'Where was this photograph taken?' I asked Alpha.

She shrugged. 'I'd never seen it before. Neither had my mother. She was in a state when she couldn't get in touch with him – I mean, now that we have the Link it's not as if we can't find anybody whenever we need to – and she went through the house trying to find some clue as to where he could have gone.

'Eventually she found an old-fashioned data storage drive hidden away in my dad's study; it was taped to the bottom of his desk. It's an antique – the drive, I mean, not the desk. We were surprised it still held data. The only thing on it was this picture.

'My dad never hides anything away; what you see is what you get with him. But he hid this, and then he disappeared. It makes no sense. My mum vaguely remembered that this photo was taken just after Dad graduated – when he was an information technologist on some special project.

'Don't you think it's a real coincidence that your father is in the photo too?'

'My mother used to say that a coincidence was just what we called events that we hadn't seen the connection between yet,' I said.

'Sounds like your mother had read the Kyle Straker Tapes,' Alpha said. 'When Kyle reaches the silos on the outskirts of Millgrove he makes a very similar observation.'

I gave her a quizzical look.

'Do you know anything about Strakerites?' she asked.

'Only what I hear from my father,' I said.

She frowned. 'Maybe not the best source. Strakerites believe that Kyle Straker existed. He was a boy who lived a long, long time ago. He watched on as the whole of the human race was upgraded by unknown forces, but remained untouched by the programming.'

'I've heard that much,' I said. 'I just couldn't really make the leap to believing it.'

Alpha winced.

'The Straker Tapes are only the start of the journey,' she continued. 'But it's not just blind faith in an unprovable proposition – there's a lot of evidence to back it up.'

'My father would disagree,' I told her.

'Yeah, well, he probably has his reasons.' Alpha disconnected filament networking abruptly. 'Look, maybe this was a bad idea.'

'What was a bad idea?' I asked, suddenly feeling like I'd upset her.

'Asking you for help. You are, I guess, your father's son.'

'That's hardly my fault,' I argued. 'Yes, he raised me, but I'm not the same as him.'

'You sounded like you thought I was insane for believing

in Kyle Straker though,' she said.

'OK, I'm sorry about that,' I replied. 'I have been raised to believe that science shows the way forward and that Strakerites are trying to drag humanity back to a dark age of superstition. I'm completely open to hearing another side of things. And I didn't mean to make out that you were crazy, it's just hard to fight against . . .'

'Your father's programming?' Alpha finished, and she actually smiled. 'I think you might be surprised by how much science Strakerites employ in their attempts to make sense of the words of Kyle Straker.'

I felt the tickle of her filament against my hand and linked back. The photograph reappeared in front of us.

Alpha pointed at the line of men, or rather at the white coats the men were wearing, and I could see an indistinct crest or logo on the breast pocket of each coat.

Alpha did an 'expand' gesture with her thumb and forefinger and the image zoomed in, on to the pocket of my father's lab coat.

Thanks to the image's fractal compression the tiny details of the zoomed image were stored along with the larger ones, and the blow-up of the pocket was sharp and clear.

There was a design that looked like a snake. The snake seemed to be eating its own tail.

Beneath it, in embroidered lettering, were the words:

Committee for the Scientific

Investigation of the Straker Tapes.

'The Doomsday Clock'

I saw the people in the crowd, all of them, and

they had become . . . were becoming . . .

something else. *Something . . . impossible.*

Rodney Peterson

interlogue

File: *224/09/12fin*

Source: *LinkData\LinkDiary\Live\Peter_Vincent\Personal*

<RUN>

We never actually stood a chance.

Our lives were mapped out for us even before we were born and there was no hope that we would ever break free of our destinies.

I even thought that I could swap courses and learn about literature.

One of the stories my mother used to read to me was about Chicken Licken. She used to do all the voices for all the animals that Chicken Licken enlisted in his mission to see the king. He had to see the king, you see, because he thought that the acorn that hit him on the head was a piece of the sky.

I guess I'm a bit like Chicken Licken, you know.

I am the boy running around trying to tell the world that the sky is falling.

And you know what? It's not an acorn this time.

The sky really is falling in.

-1-

File: *113/47/04/cbt/Continued*

Source: *LinkData\LinkDiary\Peter_Vincent\Personal*

<LinkDiary Running>

The bottom of my world didn't quite drop out, but it suddenly got a lot shakier beneath my feet.

A photograph that proved my father was on a committee that had studied the Straker Tapes?

That was like finding a photograph of Charles Darwin, hidden away in a secret laboratory, creating a monkey out of clay, or something.

All I could think of was that the photo *must* have been faked.

I mean, my father, DAVID VINCENT, undertaking a scientific study of Strakerism? He would never be a part of such a thing.

Would he?

Not the David Vincent I knew. He *hated* Strakerites.

He despised the fact that their beliefs were given any weight in this world of ours.

So to suggest that my father had ever taken their ideas *seriously*...

I tried to turn my questions into something we could use and the picture that Mr Del Rey had hidden beneath his desk seemed a good place to start.

'The people in this picture – what else do you know about them?' I said.

Alpha shook her head. 'Nothing. My mother remembered a couple of the names, the others I got because they were meta-tagged into the photo. Then I searched the Link with the names and found out about the disappearances and the suicide.'

'Hmm,' I said, 'but they must have families. Can we find them, talk to them?'

'Sure,' Alpha said. 'But why? What help can they be?'

'I don't know. I guess I need to know whether they have anything *else* in common, apart from this photograph. Are the people who disappeared all Strakerites? Did they say they felt they were being followed too? What have the families done to find the missing people? And, most importantly, what did the committee find out?'

'You can ask your father . . .'

'Yeah, I'm just not sure that is such a good idea. Not yet, anyway.'

I didn't want to talk to him until I had more information. It could be a dangerous way to proceed – if everyone else on that photo was either missing or dead, then I had to at least *warn* my father – but I needed to find more information before approaching him.

Gather supporting evidence.

Test and retest the hypothesis.

Scientific rigour: my father would expect nothing less.

And he had to be safe inside our house – the security fence would surely keep anyone out who meant him any harm.

'Are you suggesting that we play detective?' Alpha asked, grinning at the idea.

'I guess I am,' I said.

'You're full of surprises, Peter. I'm glad I called you.'

'Me too. This must be horrible for you.'

'It was,' Alpha said. 'But I feel better doing something about it. People don't just disappear, they have to be somewhere.'

The brain makes some weird connections. Something about her last sentence made me remember the Grabowitz photos.

'People don't disappear,' I said. 'But they've been *appearing* recently.'

Alpha raised an eyebrow.

I told her about the pictures that Perry had sent me, and she asked to have a look.

She frowned at the photographs for a while. 'It's weird,' she said. 'And it's another of those coincidences.'

'What is?' I asked.

'Have you ever heard of the nought-point-four?' she asked me.

I nodded. It rang a bell somewhere.

'It's a Strakerite thing, isn't it?' I asked.

She sat there a while, looking at the pictures. Her pupils were reduced to pinpricks.

'I need to tell you the story of Kyle Straker,' she said. 'I know that it's going to sound a little . . . *out there*, but I want you to keep an open mind.'

'I'll try.'

'That's all I can ask.'

She sat there a while longer, gathering her thoughts, and then she began.

<LinkDiary Suspend>

<Initiate Recording Mode>

-2-

File: *113/47/04/cbt/Continued*

Source: *LinkData\LinkDiary\Peter_Vincent\Personal*

<LinkDiary Running>

>● Record . . .

'The Straker Tapes tell us that a long time ago, the world was a completely different place from the one we live in today.

'This was a time before the Link, before filament networking, before bioluminescence and free renewable energy and World Government and any of the things we now take pretty much for granted.

'New Cambridge was just 'Cambridge' then. There were villages surrounding it that have been swallowed up and are just parts of the city now, but back then they were individual places with funny names.

'One of those villages was called Millgrove, and it is one of the most important places this world has ever known.

'But it isn't important for the usual reasons – because of any great inventions or discoveries that were made there, or any remarkable landmarks – but because of a boy called Kyle Straker, an average specimen of 21st century humanity, who was born there, and lived there for the first fifteen years of his life.

'Kyle's world had wars and famines and greed and a criminal disregard for the environment, but to Kyle it was just the way things were. He lived his life without anything remarkable happening.

'Until Kyle and his friend Lilly Dartington, and two older people – Kate O'Donnell and Rodney Peterson – were hypnotised as a part of a primitive ritual called *The Millgrove Talent Show*. When they woke up from their trances the world around them had changed.

'Everyone they knew – their family, their friends – had suddenly become *different*. To begin with, Kyle believed that everyone had been replaced by alien replicas who were no longer human.

'His tapes talk about his journey through this new world. They end with the realisation that humanity had simply been upgraded; that the changes he and his friends were seeing were the result of a new operating system for the human brain.

'And the upgrade, well, it mended the world. But it missed out Kyle and the others. A lot of others. A whole group of people who stayed at version 0.4, while the rest of the world made the leap to 1.0.

'While it was fully possible for Kyle and the other 0.4 to watch as these new people – the 1.0 – remade the world into the one that we know, it was not a two-way street. The 0.4 were inferior, and they were screened out, hidden from the eyes and minds of the 1.0.

'They became invisible to us. Still there, forbidden from using our technologies, unseen.

'I've often wondered what the nought-point-four might look like. What they might be doing now. How they might try to contact us. I'm not alone in this. Scholars have, for centuries, debated that same topic.

'The thing is, Peter, I'd say those photographs your friend sent you look pretty much like answers to me.'

> ■ *End Recording*

-3-

File: *113/47/04/cbt/Continued*

Source: *LinkData\LinkDiary\Peter_Vincent\Personal*

<LinkDiary Resume>

I listened to Alpha's alternate history lesson in silence. I wondered if what I was hearing was a new, frightening truth or just plain madness.

Truth and madness can sound pretty similar sometimes, I guess.

Yes, I *am* my father's son, and I have been raised to believe that Strakerites are – at best – dangerous eccentrics with nothing but a fictional book and a crazy set of beliefs to define them.

And yes, the story of Kyle Straker's adventures in a post-upgrade world certainly *sounded* mad, but still I wondered.

Suddenly I had a glimpse of things that might link that strange, ancient story to what I had seen today.

The ghosts in those photographs could be hoaxes, the results of data corruption . . . or could they be the remnants of a past world?

Alpha believed in the truth of the Straker Tapes, and that made me give the story a more careful consideration than I perhaps would have if I had heard it from another source.

And then there was my father.

Mysterious disappearances.

A countdown?

A suicide.

That hexing committee.

'So what do you think?' Alpha asked me, and I could tell from her face that she was filled with a whole host of thoughts and feelings that I could not read. 'What do you want to do?'

I shrugged, touched her hand and said: 'Why don't we find an address for the family of Tom Greatorex. Let's go find out what made him jump.'

-4-

File: *113/47/04/cbt/Continued*

Source: *LinkData\LinkDiary\Peter_Vincent\Personal*

<LinkDiary Running>

LinkMaps showed that the man we were interested in had lived in Ellery Tower, before he decided to take that last, lonely plunge.

According to the map it was a fifteen-minute walk, and I realised that Alpha and I were going to be skating rather too close to the edge of the curfew.

But it couldn't be helped.

We both felt the need to be doing something; hardly daring to remain still for fear that the things we were pursuing would pass from our reach.

We didn't talk a whole lot while we were walking, we were

both lost in thought.

I was still trying to work my father into the puzzle: but no matter how hard I tried, I could not believe that he had been a member of a group that had made a serious study of the Straker Tapes. Even if his conclusion was that they were fictional, they had obviously once seemed believable enough that he had afforded them the full weight of his intellect.

I checked the Link, but there was no record that I could find of the committee, or indeed its findings.

It didn't scan.

None of it scanned.

Ellery Tower was an ultra-modern sliver of glass, pointing up towards a curdled night sky. There was a dense chemical build-up in the air tonight, a by-product of our clean energy. Even though climate control keeps the skies clear during the day, at night it kind of lets the stuff do its own thing. It's harmless, but some nights it does make star gazing a little difficult.

Progress costs, it always costs, I thought, then turned my attention back to the building.

A door hissed open as we stood in front of it, and we

walked into a vast lobby with trees growing upwards into the apex of the tower barely visible overhead.

There was an *auto da fé*™ to access the upper tiers, so we walked towards the exact middle of the lobby, stepped on to the target square etched into the floor, spoke the floor we needed and rose up into the air.

I don't know if it's possible to get used to being lifted up with no visible means of support, no visible safety equipment, no sense of any mechanism or even a floor.

You seem to be breaking a law of physics just using one, but that's an illusion, of course; I guess that's how they got the name – *auto da fé*: an act of faith – because it feels like one. OK, it's a faith in science and engineering, but it feels like . . . I don't know . . . *magic*, I suppose.

We stopped on the 24th floor and stepped off on to the gantry, then made our way to apartment 9. We were at the door when we realised that neither of us had a clue how to proceed.

We were a couple of kids with no business asking anyone any questions.

We stood there until it started getting embarrassing and

then I remembered an episode from Last Quest where the warrior I was controlling needed to get some information from the Guild of Thieves. The information was about some buried treasure that I never managed to find, but what I learned was that you just needed to keep up a dialogue until you found a way to turn things around to the topic that you wanted to discuss. Of course, that was with a computer character programmed to give you the information if you used the right approach.

An actual human being had no such programming.

Still, it was better than nothing, wasn't it? So I knocked on the door.

Alpha shot me a look but I smiled to reassure her and she shrugged.

There were noises from within.

Then silence.

We had just decided that the person inside was going to ignore us when, suddenly, the door burst open.

A woman in her mid-forties stood there looking down at us. She was tall and elegant, but her eyes were dark and joyless, the flesh around them red and puffy. Her mouth was kind of twisted up in a way that reflected that inner pain.

'What is it?' she demanded, and her voice, too, was laced with sorrow. 'What do you want?'

'Ms Greatorex?' I asked, trying a warm tone. 'We need to talk to you.'

'I don't think I want to talk to anyone,' she said. 'Not now. Please, leave me alone.' She moved her hand to shut the door. 'And it's Mrs,' she added as her voice started to crack.

'I'm sorry,' I said, not sure if I was apologising for the intrusion, her grief, or for addressing her incorrectly. 'I don't want to interrupt, but we really need to talk to you. It's about Tom.'

The very mention of his name caused her face to soften. It was only a little, just a loosening of her tightened jaw muscles, but enough to give me a tiny bit of hope.

'Thomas . . .?' she said, only turning it into a question on the last syllable.

'Thomas. Yes.' I figured it might be a good idea to adopt her use of the longer form of the man's name. 'I need you to help me . . . *us.*'

I gestured at Alpha and she gave a tiny nod, solemn and earnest.

'It's my father,' Alpha said. 'He used to work with Thomas. Now he's missing. Vanished. No one has seen him.'

'Oh,' Mrs Greatorex looked confused, but her hand fell to her side and no longer looked ready to slam the door in our faces. 'Your father . . .?'

'His name is Iain, Iain Del Rey.'

'Iain?' The woman's face looked puzzled. 'Iain was the name of Mr Peterson's son.'

I looked at Alpha, primarily to pull a face that meant I thought the woman was losing it, but Alpha frowned at me.

'That's right,' Alpha said warmly. 'Iain was four years old when he developed leukaemia, and Mr Peterson made Mr Peebles to get him to laugh.'

The woman nodded, and I saw a miraculous thing. Her mouth finally untwisted and became a smile. Not much of a smile, but a smile nonetheless.

She looked at Alpha with something like admiration.

'Please,' Mrs Greatorex said. 'Won't you come inside?'

We followed her and she led us through a huge minimalist

hall lined with marble tiles. There were five doors along the hall, and she took us into the closest room. It was a lounge featuring the same lack of decor, with no seating: just four silver vents of differing sizes on the floor.

Mrs Greatorex gestured to the larger of the vents, while she went towards a smaller one, then sat down. She hung in mid-air as if there was a chair underneath her.

The seats were an act of faith, too.

I had to lower myself down and hope that there was something there to catch me, half-expecting to hit the floor with a thump.

But, just as I reached the point-of-no-return and would have found it hard to stop myself, I felt my body come into contact with something . . . *soft*.

It was so weird.

I realised that there had to be some sort of controlled blast of air coming up through the vent, forming a kind of cushion of pressure that was strong enough to support my weight, and focused enough so that it fit to the contours of my body perfectly.

It was, I was surprised to discover, incredibly comfortable.

And slightly warm.

Alpha said: 'Wow.'

I nodded in agreement.

Mrs Greatorex waved a hand in the air. 'Thomas designed the seating, because it tied in with the invisible way that makes the *auto da fé* work,' she said. 'He did so love to link things together, develop themes . . . He never stopped, you see. Even when they took it all away from him . . .'

'Who took what?' Alpha asked. 'I mean, we don't know anything about Thomas, we just found a photograph of him in my father's study . . .'

Mrs Greatorex frowned.

'My husband is . . . *was* . . . a remarkable man,' she said. 'Truly remarkable. He had a great mind, an uncommon, brilliant mind. He was able to turn himself to any problem and see through the most complex sets of data to find the simple answer that everyone else missed.

'He saw patterns that no one else could. He would look at pages and pages of statistics and numbers and suddenly he would see order. Even when they took away his lab and his livelihood he carried on, trying to find answers to questions that no one else had thought to ask.'

Mrs Greatorex shook her head, slowly and sadly. 'He became obsessed with the Link. Not with using it, but with how it worked. He had noticed some glitches in the system and he wanted to work out how to stop them happening. That was him, really. He identified a problem and then he *had* to work out a solution.

'He ran a whole series of experiments, and then set out to find some kind of pattern; something that tied all the glitches together.

'The problem is that our minds seek out patterns. I think that Thomas became so desperate to find *something*, he started to imagine that even chaos made sense.

'He started acting strangely. He became secretive and distant. I just thought he was wrapped up in his work, but it was something else . . .

'Towards the end he got very scared. He was sure that something was happening, something that he was powerless to stop. He wouldn't talk about it . . . he couldn't . . . but it was eating him up inside. You could see it on his face. He had always been so happy and full of life, but the worry was draining the joy and life from him, and I hardly recognised him at all.'

I felt Alpha's hand squeezing my arm. Hard. I looked over but she wasn't looking at me, she was staring at Mrs Greatorex with unblinking attention and I realised that she probably wasn't even aware that she had hold of me.

'Then it got really bad,' Mrs Greatorex continued. 'He started to look at me . . . with *suspicion*. He said that I was 'one of them', that they were everywhere, that there were 'a million eyes' watching him all the time.

'Fear and anxiety overtook his mind, and the whole world became one of surveillance and conspiracy.'

She broke off and I could see how much it had hurt when her husband's suspicions turned to her, implicating her in his elaborate fantasy. But what if it hadn't been a fantasy?

Because the people connected to Thomas Greatorex *had* disappeared, and that had to mean something, didn't it?

'So you're absolutely sure that there was no one watching him?' I asked her.

She looked genuinely surprised by the question.

'I don't see how there could have been,' she said after a

moment's thought. 'And a *million eyes* watching him all the time — that sounds like classic paranoia.'

Sometimes, I thought, *a duck is a duck*.

'Could he have meant that he was being watched *through the Link?*' Alpha suddenly asked. 'I mean that might seem like a million eyes, mightn't it?'

Mrs Greatorex's face turned pale. Her eyes moved quickly in her sockets as she tried to see a flaw in Alpha's reasoning.

'Oh,' was all she said after a few seconds.

We waited and I turned and nodded approval in Alpha's direction.

'It all sounded so mad,' Mrs Greatorex said, suddenly sounding like she was trying to convince herself rather than us. 'That would mean . . .' and she trailed off and sat there in shocked, contemplative silence.

I knew I needed to move her on fast.

'Did you ever hear of something called the Committee for the Scientific Investigation of the Straker Tapes?' I asked.

'Of course.' The question seemed to shake Mrs Greatorex out of her silence. 'Thomas was a data analyst for the project. He looked at all the results of the enquiry. He wasn't allowed to discuss it, not even with me, but I know how betrayed he felt when that . . . *that man* overrode the committee's true findings.

'I think that was the beginning of the end of his career. He disagreed with the official version of things and it made it very hard for him to find employment afterwards — he was the crazy one, the one who believed in the Straker Tapes . . .'

'He wasn't alone,' Alpha said. 'My father worked on that committee. He believed in Kyle, too.'

I felt a coldness in my spine.

'You said "that man".' I said. 'Who were you talking about?'

Mrs Greatorex's face showed contempt.

'The head of the committee,' she said, her lips pursed. 'The chairman. He stole my husband's life from him. He said that Tom was unstable and that his conclusions were nothing short of delusional.'

She squeezed her eyes shut and spat the next two words out with such venom that I felt ashamed and terrified.

'David Vincent.'

-5-

File: *113/47/04/cbt/Continued*

Source: *LinkData\LinkDiary\Peter_Vincent\Personal*

<LinkDiary Running>

We talked for a little while after that, but Mrs Greatorex started repeating herself. We tried pressing her for more information about our fathers, but apart from a deep-seated hatred directed towards mine, she didn't know, or wouldn't say, anything else of use.

I neglected to mention my relationship to the man who destroyed her husband's career, and Alpha was sensitive enough not to bring it up.

Alpha made a few more odd references to the Straker Tapes — something cryptic about someone called Danny, and a joke about a dog called Bambi – and then we were being shown out.

We were getting ever closer to the edge of curfew. I've never been out anywhere *near* curfew, and it looked possible I was going to miss it.

I told Alpha that I needed to get home, and she nodded.

'The weird thing is, I'm terrified of missing curfew, but I have no idea what would happen if I did,' she said.

I realised that she was right.

Even while I was sitting on a sofa made of air in Mrs Greatorex's place, the nagging discomfort that I would be late home was growing within me.

Now I was feeling close to panic.

'Look,' I said, 'we can pick this up in the morning. Maybe a good night's sleep will help us see some sense.'

She moved in closer to me, and her face looked pale and scared in the moonlight, but she still managed a smile.

'Thank you,' she said.

'For what?'

'For coming when I needed you.'

161

'It's like I told you,' I said, 'I like to help my friends.'

'Yeah, well this went above and beyond the call of duty.'

'Not at all,' I said.

Alpha seemed about to say something, then she raised herself up on tiptoe and kissed me.

It was on the cheek, and only lasted a couple of seconds, but it was a kiss all the same.

'We'd better get ourselves home,' she said, and it seemed like there was regret in her voice.

I could only nod.

'Fancy playing truant tomorrow?' she asked, and I nodded again. I'm rarely at a loss for words, but just then I could hardly *remember* how to speak.

'I like you Peter,' she said as she walked away. 'You've got a smart answer for everything.'

She'd already turned the corner when I realised that it was a joke.

-6-

File: *113/47/04/cbt/Continued*

Source: *LinkData\LinkDiary\Peter_Vincent\Personal*

<LinkDiary Running>

I arrived home with four whole minutes to spare.

My mind was a blizzard of thoughts, but none of them would settle and it all turned to slush.

I expected my father to be waiting for me, angry and accusing, and it was almost an anticlimax to discover that the house was as quiet as when I left it.

I made my way to my bedroom and sat at my desk, trying to figure out an angle to approach all of this from. Still my mind chattered away, non-stop, filling my head with near-meaningless static.

I took a calcium supplement and stared at my wall.

What did it all mean?

Did it mean anything at all?

I stood up and moved to a blank space of wall. I touched it and thought about Alpha's missing father. That made me think of the photograph and I opened up the image file in my head, deployed my filaments, and placed it on to the wall.

It sat there in the middle of all that empty space and I looked at it for a while, before zooming in on the insignia on the lab coats in the photo and placing that on the wall too.

I studied the design.

A snake eating its own tail.

I ran a LinkSearch and came up with a lot of hits. The design was called an *ouroboros* – which was ancient Greek for 'tail-eater', appropriately enough – and it was supposed to symbolise the idea that existence was somehow cyclical, that it constantly renewed, or recreated, itself.

I put the definition next to the insignia and thought about what it could mean.

That made me think of the Straker Tapes, and how Kyle believed that the human race was reprogrammed, by a software upgrade from . . . somewhere else.

I put the Grabowitz photographs up on the wall and studied them. Did they really show the ones left behind after the human race was upgraded? I studied the face of the young man, the one who was holding up fingers as if passing on a message. Was he photographic proof of what the Strakerites believed, or just another Link hoax?

I pulled up a LinkImage of the aftermath of Thomas Greatorex's suicide — the cordon with a crowd of people gathered around — and fixed that to the wall too.

Then I stood back and looked at the whole montage, trying to see the connections between the photographs.

As far as I could see there was only one connection.

The Straker Tapes.

Maybe it was time to actually read them.

I accessed the global bookshop and found it instantly.

It was a top seller. Up 853% in popularity in the last week.

That was a huge spike in sales by any standards.

I looked at the page and thought about it for a while, already hearing my father's furious voice in my head, and then I thought *Buy* and downloaded it anyway.

-7-

File: *113/47/04/cbt/Continued*

Source: *LinkData\LinkDiary\Peter_Vincent\Personal*

<LinkDiary Running>

I could have read it in my head, there and then, but that didn't feel right somehow, so I transferred it over to my LinkPad instead and sat down on the bed.

The liquid memory mattress adjusted to my form instantly.

I looked at the file for a while, sitting there amongst downloaded college textbooks, fantasy strategy guides and my secret stash of English literature, and I had the oddest of feelings. There was a small part of excitement — the odd thrill that comes from doing something that you KNOW your parents would not approve of.

I opened it up and started to read. Twenty minutes later I was done.

The story had been strange and disturbing, made all the more so by the sincerity with which Kyle Straker had related the peculiar events that happened on that single summer day.

I felt a weird chill when reading about the silos, but I couldn't explain why it was that bit of the story that should affect me the most.

I sat there, trying to get it all straight in my head. A story from many centuries ago, that I had been raised to regard as a fairy tale, but now looked to be the secret history of the world.

Then I messaged Alpha.

/Hi Peter./ she replied. ?What's up?

?Any sign of your father?

/No. Mum's beside herself. He's never done anything like this in all the time they have been married. I made up some explanations that sounded pathetic even to me, but she seems to have quietened down. For now./ ?Is that all you wanted?

/I just read it./ I said.

?It?

/The book./ I said. */The Straker Tapes./*

There was a moment's silence.

?What did you think?

/Well . . . I've certainly never read anything like it before./

?Which version did you read?

?Version?

/There are a few different versions of the Straker Tapes, some better than others./

?Better?

/Less . . . interfered with./ ?Did you have author's notes, footnotes, or just the pure text?

/No notes. Just the story./

/That's the way I prefer it. In later versions with notes and things the book gets a little confusing . . ./

/It wasn't confusing. But if it's true then . . . everything we think we know is a lie. I mean, all of it. I don't think I want it to be true./

/I know, but it's surprising how much evidence there is to support the tapes./

?Why isn't it common knowledge? I asked. ?I mean, something this important, it should be all over the Link, shouldn't it?

/Oh Peter, I don't think the Link is the limitless fount of knowledge that people make it out to be. I think that its information is controlled./

?By who?

/I don't know. By people who think that we'll panic if we find out the truth. Or by people with an interest in keeping things the way they are . . ./

?People like my father . . .?

/I don't know what he's up to, Peter, but yes. I think your father is somehow involved in keeping secrets./

/I've got to sleep on all of this./ I told her. /I'll meet you tomorrow./ ?Same place? ?About 9.30?

/I'll be there./

/Good night./

/Good night, Peter./

I sat there, my mind picking over the details of the book I had just read.

Kyle and Lilly and the village of Millgrove.

The end of one phase of humanity – the beginning of a brave new world.

Millgrove.

I'd never heard of it.

And that worried me.

I ran a search on Millgrove and came up with nothing.

It was like the Link didn't have any information on the place.

That's the way it should have been, of course, if the story was pure invention. There would be no Millgrove because it never existed in the first place; nowhere except in Kyle Straker's imagination.

But.

But.

But.

Kyle Straker wasn't the only person who believed in the world of the 0.4.

He recorded his story on to tapes, and those tapes were written down, and somewhere along the way between then and now the story *was* believed by others. The Strakerites.

The growing movement that was reaching what my father called 'epidemic proportions'.

So where was the *evidence* of that *epidemic* on the Link?

I widened my search to include Kyle Straker, and got a few hits but — apart from a Linkipedia entry — they were nothing more than arguments *against* Strakerism. It was as if a blanket of obscurity had been thrown over the topic, with little to be gleaned, even for the most dedicated searcher.

I put the Linkipedia entry on to my wall, and made a few notes around it, mostly about the lack of decent information on the subject. I copied some of my favourite parts of the Straker Tapes —the bits that I thought most relevant to the things that were happening today — and added them to the rest of the evidence.

Evidence.

Weird word to be using, I know, but it felt like the right one. This was turning into an investigation. There was something at work here that was so big I could only glimpse the tiniest parts of it. How those parts tied together, what they were for and what they meant, was beyond my ability to see.

And that annoyed the hex out of me.

A million eyes . . .

I suddenly remembered what Mrs Greatorex had said about her husband, about the way he became convinced that he was being watched, and I made a note of that on the wall too.

Then I sat on my bed and stared at all the data.

I felt an urgency to sort things out, was aware that a clock I couldn't see was counting down to . . .

. . . to what?

That was the question, wasn't it?

The young man in the photos counting down on his fingers — was he one of the 0.4? The 1.0? The 1.4.7?

I felt a cold trickle down the length of my spine.

Counting down on his fingers.

Was he counting down to another upgrade? I thought, suddenly. *Does everything change tomorrow?*

I stared at the wall, looking for something that would disprove the wild, insane, horrible theory.

But nothing there helped.

I lay down on my bed, with dark thoughts flowing through

my head. Outside my window I could hear the muted buzz of artificial bees.

What can I do? I asked myself. *What can any of us do?*

There was, of course, no answer.

<LinkDiary Off>

-8-

File: *113/42/01/aet*

Source: *LinkData\LinkDiary\Peter_Vincent\Dream*

<LinkDiary On>

I dreamed that I was standing in the street outside New Lincoln Heights, staring up at the crystal spires.

Except they weren't quite the spires I'd been looking at earlier.

The alien language from the Straker Tapes was writhing and curling like smoke across the crystal walls, and there was a high-pitched squeal — like the screams of a million people — tearing through the air.

Over the towers hovered dull grey clouds, and there was no sun in the sky. Everything around me looked like it had been leeched of colour, pallid shadows of their former selves.

174

The only thing unaffected by the fade-out was the horrible language that was spreading outwards from the towers, moving throughout the sky, until it infected the clouds with its alien message.

The clouds grew heavy with code, bloated and stretched, and then they let go and the code rained down on the world below.

My heart was pounding in my chest like it was trying to break free of its bone cage.

I wanted to turn away, run as far from there as was possible, but I could not move, I could only stand and watch as the wet code from the clouds splashed around me, and everything it touched became tainted by it.

I watched as a group of people fled towards me, their eyes wide in terror. The rain enveloped them and then they were being swallowed up by the hooks and eyes of that terrible code. It seemed to dance across their flesh before sinking into their bodies.

Suddenly the fear in their faces was gone, replaced by a uniform blank look. They stopped moving and stood upright, their eyes blinking in unison, and behind them the crystal towers blurred – like a graphical glitch – and then they were different: twin concrete towers, rounded at the top.

'You must not look at goblin men,' a voice behind me said, and I recognised it as Alpha's. I turned in relief and gratitude, only to see the man who'd shouted at me when I was walking back home: the goblin man himself. 'Their fruits have roots deep underground,' he said, eyes wide and hair tousled, 'where you will find a worm is eating its own tail. A place where all things begin and end. Alpha. And Omega. She'll follow you into fire, but why would you lead her there?'

'Who are you?' I asked, but my voice sounded like a child's.

The man ignored me as if he hadn't even heard.

'She wants to find her father,' he said, 'but the key is with your mother. To find him, find her. Follow the breadcrumbs. They will lead you here.' He pointed to the concrete towers.

I turned to look at the towers and when I turned back the man was gone.

There was a sound like thunder in the sky.

I turned my face up to the heavens and the clouds were gone. The alien code was gone.

And that was when I saw. That was when I saw THEM.

There were things up there, on the other side of the sky, pushed up against it and making the sky itself stretch under their pressure. It was as if the sky above me was little more than a skin, and the things were pressing against it from outside our atmosphere, making it bulge inwards.

I can't say what the creatures looked like because I only saw unrelated details. There were flexing coils that could have been ropes or tentacles or tubules, enormous and terrible. There were the gelatinous lumps and knotted bumps that pulsed against the sky, making it shake. Then there were the horrible patches that seemed to be concealing squirming masses of things that I could have thought were maggots writhing in dead flesh if it wasn't for their colossal, impossible scale.

As I watched, a tear appeared in the curdled sky, and a mass of vast, grey, wet tubing lolled obscenely from the wound in our atmosphere.

The sky is falling, *I thought as I woke up.* The sky is falling and there's nothing anyone can do to stop it.

-9-

File: *113/47/04/sfg*

Source: *LinkData\LinkDiary\Peter_Vincent\Personal*

<LinkDiary Running>

I awoke feeling tired and drained and on the very brink of panic. The terrible imagery of the dream was still clinging to my mind like cobwebs.

It was far and away the weirdest I've ever had. It took me minutes to shake free of it, but eventually it lessened its grip on me, and I was able to push it to the back of my mind and concentrate on the things that needed to be done.

I chose 'simple but sophisticated' as my wardrobe theme for the day, shut down the data wall and went out to face the world.

My father was in the dining room, reading data from a

LinkPad. He didn't so much as acknowledge my presence, so I left him to his work, fixed myself some breakfast, bolted it down and made to leave the room.

'Are you going out, Peter?' my father asked, without looking up from his Pad.

I froze, my hand on the door stud.

'I–I . . .' I started to say.

'It's all right, Peter,' he said. 'I know what you are up to. And I know that you are only playing your part in the drama of life. The question you should be asking yourself is, *who's writing the script?*'

'What are we talking about here?' I asked. 'Is this about the college course?'

Still my father studied the screen of his Pad.

'English Literature,' he said, and made it sound like a pair of dirty words. 'That's about the least of it, right, Peter?'

'If you say so,' I said.

'I certainly do say so.' There was steel in his voice, but still he didn't look up.

'I was going to tell you,' I said, pathetically.

'There's nothing to tell,' my father responded. 'Today

is going to be . . . very interesting indeed. Run around, play detective, find out the truth for yourself,' he broke off and finally looked up from his screen. 'See if it makes any difference at all.' And he grinned. 'I left something for you on the table by the front door,' he said. 'A present for you and Alpha.'

Then he looked back at his screen.

It was hard to know whether he was finished or not, but the seconds passed slowly and he didn't say anything else so I let myself out.

On the table by the door was the 'present': a small anthracite-black case with a gold hinge. I tried to open it but my hands were shaking, and to be honest I just wanted to get away from there, so I put it in my pocket and walked out.

Did my father know everything?

I felt sick and my stomach was knotted into leaden coils. Had he been reading my LinkDiary? Even though it was encrypted?

It was the only explanation I could find for the things he seemed to know.

The thought that he had broken into my LinkDiary made

me angry, but also something else.

Confused.

If he did know everything, if he knew what I was doing and where I was going, then why hadn't he told me off, grounded me, or tried to stop me?

I'd lived in such a state of anxiety about him finding out that I had enrolled on the English Literature course, and he had hardly given it a moment's thought.

He *definitely* knew about Alpha, though – which should have sent him into an incandescent rage.

But he had been calm; *resigned* almost.

Or worse, he hadn't cared.

That worried me more than anything else: his complete indifference.

LinkPeople

An Interview with David Vincent

Q. So, you are perhaps one of the best-known scientists in the world. Certainly the most high-profile. How does that feel?

A. Feel? Great, I suppose. It's odd, because history is littered with far greater scientists than me, but I'm who people immediately think of when asked to name one. And it's flattering, but humbling too.

And in all likelihood utterly undeserved.

Q. The man who saved the world from the bee crisis? Undeserving?

A. Well, that's what I mean, really. The bee crisis was a high-profile thing, and everyone was aware of it, so it was inevitable that it would be seen as a defining moment for me, but it was nowhere near as important as figuring out gravity, or DNA, or the laws of thermodynamics. I guess what I did was just a bit flashier.

Q. It was certainly that. (*Laughs.*) Anyway, you are a — how shall I put this — an outspoken opponent of Strakerite doctrine, and especially its place within our schools. What are the problems that you see in Upgradist thinking?
A. Ah, straight in with a big one.

Well, the problems are simple. You see, Strakerism is built upon an unprovable premise: that we owe our minds, our ideas, even our physical characteristics, to alien creatures; programmers from outer space; gods in all but name.

But it's nothing more than superstition. And superstition is the enemy of scientific progress, of reason. Science is based on the provable, the measurable and the repeatable. Superstition, on the other hand, requires no tests, no measurements, no proof: just faith.

It is a viewpoint that explains human existence by using a lie. A primitive, childish lie. Humanity got to be the way it is through many millions of years of the greatest scientific project this planet has ever seen: evolution.

To deny the truth of evolution by natural selection is to deny the very truth of ourselves, and that is incredibly dangerous.

Q. Right, evolution. Strakerites suggest that it's a theory that stops covering humankind hundreds of thousands of years ago, and that filament networking, the Link and other such things seemed to occur very recently and cannot be explained by evolution. How do you reply to these suggestions?

A. How does anyone reply to statements that are so wrong? The Strakerites have built themselves a 'case' on the flimsiest foundations, always demanding that we show them where 'x' came from, or when 'y' arrived as a human characteristic, without stopping to think that the alternative they suggest is, frankly, absurd. We have evidence of evolution. We have evidence that the human animal has, for millions of years, adapted to challenges that were flung its way by this planet of ours, and every time our genes have risen to the challenge.

Where, I ask them, is the evidence for these so-called alien programmers? I mean, a single, tiny shred of evidence would do for starters, wouldn't it? The problem is that incredible claims require incredible evidence, and without that evidence the Strakerite house of cards just falls down.

Why do we, as a race, constantly seek ridiculous answers to simple questions? Why would we rather believe in people from the sky? In gods and ghosts and monsters?

It makes me sad that we have come so far, that we understand so much, but would still rather put our faith in alien programmers than believe the evidence we see around us every day. Strakerites have a habit of ignoring that evidence. And that is why their doctrine CANNOT be taught in schools.

-10-

File: *113/47/04/sfg/Continued*

Source: *LinkData\LinkDiary\Peter_Vincent\Personal*

<LinkDiary Running>

Alpha was waiting for me at what I was starting to think of as our spot.

I mean how crazy is that? We'd met there once and I was already attaching sentiment to the place.

Anyway, she looked desperately glad to see me and we had an awkward sort of hug; and then I told her about my father and handed her the black case.

She frowned at it.

'What is it?' she asked.

I shrugged. 'Beats me.'

She thumbed the case open and we both stared at

what was inside.

Four small, glass discs laid out on a dark cloth.

Alpha looked puzzled. 'What on Earth are they?' she asked.

I'd seen something like them before in a science lesson. We'd been talking about medical advances, and how we no longer needed some of the things that had been important to people in the past.

The lecturer had handed around a set of small glass discs and asked everyone what they thought they were.

No one had known.

Inside the box my father had given me were two pairs of those same glass discs.

'People used to put these on their eyes,' I told her. 'They were used to correct defects in sight, before we learned that our filaments were perfectly capable of adjusting our vision. They were called *contact lenses*.'

A memory surfaced, and I replayed the odd moment in the car when my father looked over at me and his eyes had changed from blue to brown.

Here was the explanation.

He'd been wearing contact lenses.

Just like these.

Alpha looked at me in confusion. 'What an odd gift,' she said. 'My vision is perfect. Yours?'

'As good as it's ever needed to be,' I said. 'They must be fashion accessories. He's started wearing them, to change the colour of his eyes, but I wonder why he gave them to *us*.'

'I wonder how he *knew* there was an *us*,' Alpha reflected. She snapped the case shut and handed it back to me. 'I've hardly slept. But I had a few thoughts on some people we can speak to. If you still want to?'

'Of course I do. I've had a few ideas of my own.'

'A couple of soys while we compare notes?' Alpha asked, smiling. 'My treat.'

'You're on,' I said, pocketing the case that my father had given me.

'I know a place,' Alpha said, 'close to here, but a little off the beaten track.'

'Let's go,' I told her.

A few hundred yards and a couple of side streets later we were standing in front of a gloomy looking little building on a street of gloomy looking buildings. Weirdly, I'd never ventured off the main beltways and slidewalks, so I had only ever seen the shops and buildings that advertised the new world we were living in: the ones with neon and poured granite; plasteel and plexiglass.

Far from the usual hi-tech, sparkling shops I was used to seeing, these ones looked like they belonged in the pages of a history book. They seemed to have been built of original materials that I had only ever read about.

Concrete and brick.

And the weirdest thing? They were three storeys high.

Not twenty or thirty like the buildings that hemmed this strange little street in on all sides.

In a place where living space was at a premium, where the only way to find new real estate was by building upwards, it seemed inconceivable that this place hadn't been demolished for more space-effective developments.

It was like stepping into another time period.

'Welcome to *my* world,' Alpha said, indicating the row of shops with an expansive sweep of the hand. She must have seen the look on my face because she followed it with: 'Not quite what you're used to, Peter?'

'I didn't know there were streets like this left in New Cambridge,' I confessed.

'People choose not to see them,' Alpha said. 'Some Strakerites even believe that these are the kind of places that Kyle talks about on the tapes — places that have become irrelevant to the upgraded masses.'

I raised an eyebrow.

'You've got to admit,' she said, 'they really shouldn't be here.'

She smiled and pointed to a door handle.

'So how about this soy, then?' she asked.

The door opened and there was an odd, metallic tinkling sound. I looked up and saw there was a small metal bell at the top of the door, triggered to ring when it was opened.

'A Straker-themed place?' I asked with a laugh, remembering the bell in the Happy Shopper in Millgrove, and how Kyle Straker had thought it out-dated and old-fashioned even then.

Alpha smiled, but it was a bit thin. I guess I was kind of attacking her beliefs by making light of them.

The café we walked into could have been a museum exhibit. My shoes squeaked on boards underfoot, and looking around at the furniture I realised that we were surrounded by wood.

We have a few window frames made out of wood at home, and I know that my father paid a whole lot of money to acquire them, and called in a favour or two to get the necessary permits. To him, I'm sure, wood is nothing more than a status symbol, something to flaunt his wealth and power.

Here, in this weird café on a street that shouldn't even exist, people sat on chairs and stools made entirely of the stuff; they put plates and cups and cutlery *directly* on to the surfaces of wooden tables. They even walked on wood as they moved about the room.

There was a literal *fortune* in the stuff; but here it wasn't displayed for people to admire as a luxury item or status symbol, but rather was a practical material to be used and enjoyed.

I couldn't believe it.

Alpha waited patiently by my side for me to take it all in.

'What do you think?' she asked.

'It's . . . incredible,' I said quietly.

She nodded. 'Incredible will do,' she said and marched up to the counter. I followed along in her wake, feeling out of place and out of my depth.

I'd spent my whole life thinking that the world was one way, and then in the space of a day or two I'd discovered that maybe I was wrong. I'd spent too much time believing the words of others, and not enough time opening my eyes and just looking at what was really around me.

It made me feel . . . well, kind of an ass, if I'm honest.

It was no real surprise that the man behind the counter seemed to know Alpha pretty well. He smiled a big, warm smile and knew exactly what she wanted before she had to order. Alpha held up two fingers and the man nodded, turned his attention to me and raised an eyebrow before looking back at Alpha. She nodded, he shrugged and then he went out the back, returning after a few moments with two glasses of pinkish liquid.

Glasses.

As in 'made of glass'.

Not plastic, or paper, or some new polymer that all this year's must-have items were made of.

Glass.

Alpha tried to flash him some cash, but the man shook his head.

'You brighten the place up,' he said. 'That's payment enough.'

Alpha thanked him and we found ourselves a table in the corner of the room.

The place was small and very busy, but it was a friendlier sort of busy than I'm used to. The air was full of fruity smells mixed with polish and antiquity. There were no tense faces or grudging expressions from people who didn't want to be pressed in so close to other people.

And no one seemed lost in their own Link activity.

I liked it immediately.

I sipped my drink and was startled to discover that it was probably one of the most delicious things I had ever tasted. Not like a normal soy at all. Sweet, but with a surprising natural sharpness.

'It's made with *real* raspberries,' Alpha explained. 'Not the mass-produced GM things that get passed off as raspberries these days, but the real thing. Grown just like they were in the olden days.

'What is this place?' I asked her. 'I mean, what . . . how . . .?'

I was full of questions, but Alpha didn't seem to mind. She sipped her raspberry drink and then started talking.

'Most people would be as shocked as you are to find out places like this exist,' she said. 'To them Strakerites are nothing more than superstitious fools. But whatever you might have heard, Strakerites have a simple belief that underpins everything we do: that this world we live in is not the one that we are supposed to occupy; that every time humanity is upgraded it loses something . . . *vital* . . . in the process.'

She gestured around her.

'Places like this try to recreate the world as we think it should *really* be; to bring ourselves closer to what the world would be if it wasn't for the constant interference of those alien programmers.

'So we use books and video files of things as they once were, and we try to live the *old* way. We use old technologies and old things. To better understand ourselves as *separate* from the programmers.

'To work out who we would be, if things were different.' She broke off and rolled her eyes.

'It's OK,' I told her. 'I really don't mind. I want to know all about you . . . er . . . all about Strakerites . . .'

My last minute revision was so obvious, so blatant, that I stared down at the table top and tried to will my face not to blush with embarrassment.

Alpha looked at me and I could see a tinge of sorrow in her eyes. 'It must be hard being David Vincent's son,' she said.

'I don't know what it would be like to be anyone else.'

'Until the next upgrade,' Alpha said solemnly. 'So, is there a Mrs Vincent?'

'No, I never married.'

She swatted my arm. 'Very funny. I meant your mother . . .'

'I know,' I said. 'And I deflected your question with some sparkling wit. It's called a defence mechanism.'

Alpha arched an eyebrow, surprised that I should remember her words of the day before so clearly.

'My mother . . .' I stammered, searching for the right words, 'my mother is no longer with us.'

'Oh, I'm sorry, Peter, I didn't mean to . . .'

'It's OK,' I told her. 'I was a little kid when it happened.'

'So what *did* happen?' There was a softness to Alpha's question that made me feel that I could actually talk about it, perhaps for the first time ever. I mean, I don't even think I've talked about it in my LinkDiary before.

But Alpha had asked and I suddenly flashed on the dream I'd had, the strange man talking to me just before the sky fell in.

She wants to find her father, he had said, *but the key is with your mother.*

'Let me show you,' I said, and extended my hand towards hers, placing it on the table.

She hesitated for a couple of seconds then laid her hand flat on the table in front of her, next to mine.

We let our filaments out, and the glistening ropes met, joined and merged.

I accessed deep memory storage and selected the file.

-11-

File: *040/7/113/mother*
Source: *LinkData\LinkDiary\Deep_Storage\key_memory*

<Play Memory>
<LinkDiary On>

I am eight years old.

I'm in the garden, watching the bees.

And I am recording it straight on to the Link.

They fascinate me, the bees; they always have.

It's the way that they seem to be living creatures, even though I know that they aren't.

I mean they move and fly and buzz and – occasionally – swarm, and if you sit and watch them you can see them do something that looks too much like play to be anything that could have been programmed into their circuits.

I'm watching two of them as they perform a sort of dance on the leaves of a flower in the garden. One is circling around in a clockwise direction, shaking its body every few seconds or so; the other is moving anticlockwise and seems to be echoing the shakes of its companion.

I think they are talking.

Communicating.

And I'm wondering just what it is that synthetic bees have to talk about.

A gentle hand on my shoulder pulls me out of my thoughts. The hand squeezes and I know it is my mother without turning around. My father doesn't do shows of affection.

I turn around and there she is, my mother, and the way she's standing – in front of a blazing sun – makes it seem like there's a halo of light surrounding her.

I feel myself smile.

She is my world, I think, and it makes me feel safe.

And then I notice something.

My mother is not smiling.

She is just standing there, looking down at me, her

edges blurred by the brightness of the sun, and her face looks . . . sad. As if she is on the edge of tears.

I'm wondering what it is that I have done to make her look so upset, but then she is swooping down and wrapping me up in her arms and I feel her breath on my face and feel her tears on my cheek and she holds me for a long time and I can hear the bees buzzing and feel her heart beating against me and I know that it's not me that has made her sad, but that I am somehow the focus of her sadness.

'Mummy?' I say, and I feel her whisper against my ear in reply.

'I love you, Peter,' she says, little more than a soft breath made into words by the shaping of her lips. 'If you remember nothing else, remember that.'

I touch her hair and it feels like silk, looks like spun gold in the sunlight. I can feel more of her tears, and I don't know what to do, what to say.

Parents are supposed to make a child's tears go away, and I am overwhelmed by the discovery that they can cry themselves.

I hold on to her for a long time, and then she ruffles my

hair, releases me from her hug. She looks down at me, her face filled with sorrow, with regret. Then she bends down and kisses my cheek, stands up, turns and walks away.

The sound of bees is the soundtrack to her departing.

There is a shimmer, like a mirage, a trick of the light, and I am momentarily blinded.

By the time my vision clears, my mother is gone.

-12-

File: *113/47/04/sfg/Continued*
Source: *LinkData\LinkDiary\Peter_Vincent\Personal*

<LinkDiary Running>

I let the memory run its course and then retracted my filaments. I wasn't surprised to find that there were tears in my eyes.

I rarely visit that memory.

It hurts too much.

That was, after all, the last time I saw my mother.

Alpha was studying my face, looking confused.

'I — I don't understand,' she said. 'That was the last time you saw her?'

I nodded. It was all that I could manage by way of reply.

'Where . . . where did she go?' Alpha's voice was quiet, but there was a tension to it, too, as if she wasn't quite satisfied by the contents of the memory I had shown her.

I shrugged. 'My father said that she left us. That she no longer wanted to be with us. That she had other places she wanted to see, other things she wanted to do, and those plans just didn't include a family.

'I never understood. I still don't. I've spent the last seven years wondering what could have been so important that she walked out on her own son. She loved me; at least, I think she did.'

Alpha stroked the back of my hand with her fingertips.

'What else does your father say about it?' she asked.

I shook my head. 'He's never spoken about it since that day,' I told her. 'He's not really the type to talk about feelings and stuff. I guess it's too painful for him.

'You know the stupid thing? For the first year or so there wasn't a day that passed that I wasn't thinking about her, hoping to see her face in a crowd, hoping to get a LinkMessage from her telling me she was OK. Anything.

'But as time passed I started to think about her less and

less. Now I can only remember her face if I look at stored memories.'

Alpha's face was creased with concern. She was frowning and I had a sudden horrible thought that I had upset her somehow by showing her the memory. Then her expression changed, and there was a sudden intensity to it.

'Hey, Peter,' she said. 'You blame yourself, don't you?'

'Why else would she go?' I asked. 'I must have done something . . .'

'You didn't,' Alpha said and her certainty startled me. 'Look, I don't know if this will help, but there was something . . . *wrong* with that memory.'

'What do you mean?'

'I'm not one hundred per cent certain, but something makes me think that we didn't see the whole thing.'

'That's all I've got,' I said, feeling a sudden flash of anger at the suggestion that I could be holding something back from her.

'Maybe.' Alpha stood up. 'But I reckon we need to find ourselves the services of a decent hacker to be certain.

Wait here.'

I watched her as she went over to the man at the counter. She chatted with him for a while and then he nodded and pointed to a woman at a table on the other side of the room. Alpha approached her, had another conversation, and then the woman looked over at me.

She followed Alpha back to the table where I was sitting.

'Peter, right?' The woman said as Alpha took her seat in front of me.

The woman continued to stand. She was tall and thin and had a narrow, wary face, topped off with a brief scrub of black hair. Her eyes were dark and locked on to mine.

I nodded. 'Peter Vincent.' I said.

'Hey, Peter Vincent,' the woman said. 'I'm Ashley.' She cracked a wide smile and sat down. 'You ever hacked your own code before?' she asked.

I shook my head. 'I'm not even sure what that is,' I confessed.

'That's fine. Just think of it as gaining access to things you know subconsciously. We are creatures of data, but we rarely take the time to analyse any of the information that flows through us. Which is kind of stupid, right? I'm going to help you do just that. You up for it?'

I looked at Alpha and she gave me an encouraging nod. 'Sure,' I said. 'What do I have to do?'

-13-

File: *113/47/04/sfg/Continued*

Source: *LinkData\LinkDiary\Peter_Vincent\Personal*

<LinkDiary Running>

Ashley went away into a back room but returned quickly with a wooden box.

She placed it in the middle of the table, flipped open the top, and revealed a cone-shaped device festooned with wires and circuits. Some of the wires terminated in flat plates of shining metal. It all had an odd, homemade look that made me think that the woman was playing some kind of joke or trick.

She put the wooden box on the floor under the table and then gestured at the cone.

'This is what we call a LinkCrawler,' she explained. 'It's not the best name ever, but what the hex. We use them to hack into our own operating systems. It's pretty new tech, and we haven't got it *all* worked out yet, but it allows a person to look at the code for the software that we're running.' She noticed my disbelieving look.

'I'm not kidding you,' she said, somewhat defensively. 'It's not something we're particularly good at reading yet, but there's definitely code.' She shrugged and then grinned. 'It's a total blast, by the way.'

I stared at the object on the table. It looked kinda stupid.

'Now Alpha was saying that this is a rather . . . emotional memory for you,' Ashley continued. 'You sure you don't mind if a complete stranger joins in?'

I shook my head. 'Alpha also said she thinks there might be some data missing from the memory,' I told her. 'I'm pretty keen on finding out if she's right.'

Alpha gave me a smile, warm and encouraging.

'OK,' Ashley said, as she moved wires on the LinkCrawler, performing some final adjustments. 'The Link pulls data from loads of sources, and it's doing it all of the time. Much of that time we don't even realise it's doing anything at all.

It even runs while we sleep. Do you want to know the weirdest thing, Peter? We are the most curious creatures this planet has ever known, we have discovered the secrets of the atom, taken ourselves into space in search of answers out there, we have plumbed the deepest depths of the planet's oceans, and yet we don't ask questions about the Link. About what it is, what it does, whether we even need it in our lives . . .'

'Or how it works?' I said.

Ashley raised an eyebrow. 'Yes, that's the BIG question that no one asks,' she said. 'That no one dares to ask. Because it shouldn't work, should it? The Link happened pretty much overnight,' she continued. 'There was no sudden technological breakthrough, no patent was ever filed, there are no records of the commercial development of this world-changing technology. It just happened. Like we woke up one day and the Link was suddenly there. We could communicate across vast distances with nothing but our minds to make it happen.

'Have you read the Straker Tapes?'

'Last night,' I said. 'Kind of eye-opening.'

'So you know the odd things that Kyle said towards the

end of his account? About how the unknown programmers were upgrading humanity for purposes of their own? That they were networking us as storage space . . .'

'And you think that the Link might be a result of that networking?' I asked.

Ashley looked impressed. 'Think about how the people in the later stages of Kyle's account seemed linked together. Maybe networking is necessary — not to us, but to our programmers.

'Humanity, however, just came along and did what it always does: it took advantage of an existing resource. I think that the Link is a use we found for it.'

She finished tinkering with the device and smiled.

'All done,' she said. 'You ready to give this a try?'

I nodded.

'Smart AND brave.' Ashley smiled a reassuring smile. 'Just put your hand on the table,' she instructed. 'You too, Alpha.' We both did as we were told. 'Link up, folks.' We all deployed our filaments. 'Now connect yourselves up to a platen . . .'

I stared at her.

'One of the flat metal plates,' Ashley explained.

The metal was warm and vibrated as the connection was made. Alpha and Ashley linked up to it too.

'Alpha says that she felt something odd about this memory file from the outset,' Ashley said. 'So why don't we start at the very beginning?'

I nodded, accessed the file, and it played through again.

-11 (part 2)-

File: *040/7/113/mother*
Source: *LinkData\LinkDiary\Deep_Storage\key_memory*

<Play Memory>
<LinkDiary On>

I am eight years old.

I'm in the garden, watching the bees.

And I am recording it straight on to the Link.

They fascinate me, the bees, they always have.

It's the way that they seem to be living creatures, even though I know that they aren't.

I mean they move and fly and buzz and – occasionally – swarm, and if you sit and watch them you can see them do something that looks too much like play to be anything that could have been programmed into their circuits.

I'm watching two of them as they perform a sort of dance on the leaves of a flower in the garden. One is circling around in a clockwise direction, shaking its body every few seconds or so; the other is moving anticlockwise and seems to be echoing the shakes of its companion.

I think they are talking.

Communicating.

And I'm wondering just what it is that synthetic bees have to talk about.

<Wait a minute: pause this here, can you?> Ashley says, and I halt the memory. <That's good, don't lose it, just hold it steady.>

I do as she says, and keep the memory frozen like a still picture. It just takes a little concentration.

Ashley says: <This can't be right.>

<What?> I ask.

<Well, first off: 'I am eight years old'.> Ashley says. <That's how the memory starts, isn't it?>

<Er, y-e-es.> I say, slightly patronisingly.

<The rest of the memory is not in an eight year old's

212

syntax.> Ashley says. <It's not the way an eight year old talks.> she explains before I ask. <And there's something here . . . the bees . . . I mean it's not possible, is it? Here, let me try something.>

The bees, I think, *what is she talking about?*

I'm about to ask her, but suddenly I feel her presence on the wires like an electrical current passing through me, and the next thing I know she is stepping into the memory itself.

One second I'm looking at my treasured memory, and the next . . . she's in it.

Standing there. In *my* memory.

I can see her, just off to the side of that long-past me. She is looking around sort of absently. The rest of the image is frozen, but she is moving around it. All of a sudden I'm reminded of the Straker Tapes, and of Kyle and Lilly moving around the village green while the rest of the villagers are frozen.

Weird.

Suddenly she kneels down. She is concentrating on the dance of the bees.

<Come in.> she says. <Just think about entering the

memory, and it will happen. Both of you.>

I concentrate on doing exactly as I am instructed and feel an odd tension, as if I am pushing against a solid surface, and then there's some give and suddenly I am standing next to Alpha and Ashley . . .

And me.

. . . and a small boy . . .

It's me!

. . . who is studying the bees as they dance across the leaves of a flower.

The light is almost too real to be real.

Hyper-real.

It's bright and warm and I can feel the sun of that long gone day beating down upon me. I'm supposed to be sitting in a dark little café and I still feel the urge to shade my eyes.

<Pretty weird, huh?> Ashley says, and I can only just manage a nod.

Although 'weird' is not a strong enough word to describe this. I've been using it already.

Weirdest, perhaps.

<Peter?> Ashley says. <Meet . . . well, Peter.>

She points to the boy — *to me!* — and I feel my head start to struggle with the situation.

<How?> I ask. <I . . . shouldn't he . . . how can I . . .?>

<That's kinda the point here.> Ashley says. <I guess you need to work it all out for yourself. Have a look around.>

So I do. In a daze.

I am walking around my own memory.

Like I've travelled back in time seven years.

I can see the boy as clearly as I have ever seen anything. His face is a little fatter than mine is now, and the hair a little curlier, but it is unmistakeably *me*.

<Ask the question.> Ashley says.

I don't have to ask her what she is talking about. There's a leaden feeling in my stomach and my mind is fizzing with the impossibility of what I am seeing.

<It doesn't makes sense.> I tell her. <I recorded this memory to the Link, just like I always do . . .>

<So?>

<So how can I see ME?> I say breathlessly. <I should just see what I saw, but there's no way I could *see* me *seeing* it. I . . . I shouldn't be there. I should be seeing this from that little boy's point of view. How is this possible?>

<I think it's what tipped off Alpha,> Ashley replies. <The answer is: I don't think this is *entirely* your own memory of the event. Someone else has constructed this for you. They've used enough of your own thoughts to give the feeling of it being yours, but it's a fabrication. A cut and paste job made up of your memories and someone else's.>

<Why would someone go to that trouble?>

<Another good question. Maybe we should investigate. Have a look around for clues.>

I can only nod. My mouth is completely dry and I feel like someone has pulled the world out from underneath my feet.

If I can no longer trust the evidence of my LinkDiary, then how can I trust anything?

So I search around the scene of that painful, wonderful memory looking for signs that it is constructed. Looking for things that don't fit.

I look at the boy that I once was, his brow creased as he tries to figure what it is the bees are trying to tell him . . .

<That's it,> Ashley says. <What are the bees trying to tell him? Or, more crucially, what are they trying to tell you?>

Bees? What are the bees saying? She's . . . oh wait, this is messed up.

The rest of the memory is frozen still, like a moment trapped in Lucite, but the bees are still moving! And I realise that they're not humming, they're not buzzing, they're . . .

They're talking.

They are talking to each other.

It sounds like voices overheard from a long way away: I can't hear the actual words, but I do recognise them as words.

I kneel down next to that young Peter, his face frozen as he too studies the bees. It feels so utterly strange, to be so close to a past version of me, and I find I have to just kind of ignore him.

Ignore *me*.

Or go mad.

And the bees *are* moving, but not in an ordinary bee-like

217

pattern. Their metal and plastic bodies are smooth and clean, but there is something very odd . . . very *sinister* . . . in what they are doing. They seem to be winking in and out of existence as they move, disappearing here, reappearing over there, as if there is some sort of a graphical glitch in the memory file.

I can hear them clearly now.

. . . *I don't understand,* one bee is saying. *You're scaring me, Mummy.*

I have to go away, the other bee replies. *I just have to, that's all.*

But . . . I . . . I need you, Mummy. It's my voice, from the past.

I've never heard this part of the memory before.

I need you to be strong, my mother's voice tells me, and I feel the tears welling up in my eyes at the sound of her voice. It sounds so sad, so full of regret.

Mummy! I hear myself shout. *Mummy. Don't go. Please.*

I have to. I love you, Petey, always remember that. I'm doing this . . . I'm doing this for you. For all the children like you. I . . . I have to go, Petey. I have to go back.

Go back? *I think.* Go back where? What is she talking about?

The bees are moving normally now, they are no longer appearing and disappearing, they are just moving in their incomprehensible dance across the leaves in the garden.

<Peter?> someone asks me, and I realise that it is Alpha. She is next to me in the memory, and she puts her hand on to my shoulder.

It restarts the memory.

A gentle hand on my shoulder pulls me out of my thoughts. The hand squeezes and I know it is my mother without turning around. My father doesn't do shows of affection.

I turn around and there she is, my mother, and the way she's standing – in front of a blazing sun – makes it seem like there's a halo of light surrounding her.

<Freeze it. Freeze it there.> Ashley tells me and I do just as she says. The memory once more becomes a still frame.

I am overwhelmed with a sense of loss. I mean, it's a miracle that I am here, standing so close to her, but it's just

219

a reminder of everything that I lost when she walked out of our garden seven years ago . . .

<I don't think she did,> Ashley says and I realise that I am broadcasting my thoughts. <Take a look at her. I mean take a really close look at her. And pay attention to the edges.>

The edges? What the hex is she talking about . . .

Oh, wait.

Now that is odd.

I move closer and I see immediately what Ashley is talking about. The edges of my mother are hazy, strange, and it looks like she is an image that has been . . . cut away from its background.

Like the memory itself has been . . . *edited.*

<That's right.> Ashley says. <I don't think that *this* is *really* where this scene took place.>

I reach out my hand and touch the tattered edges of my mother's image. Here, up close, it's so obvious that the memory has been tampered with. I can even feel the edit marks tingle in my fingertips as I touch them, like tiny electric shocks.

I realise that Ashley is right, and just about everything about this memory is a lie.

This is the most important memory that I have, I think, *and it's not even real.*

I feel a blood-red anger that boils inside me.

<Can we reconstruct the true memory?> I demand, urgently. <Is there any way . . .?>

<Way ahead of you there,> Ashley says, and there is a lightness in her voice that puzzles me. She sounds like she's enjoying this . . . This is just a technical problem for her to solve, and she must like solving problems.

<There's not enough data in the edits around your mother, but . . .>

<But?>

<Well, I'm thinking about the bees again,> Ashley tells me. <I don't believe that the conversation we overheard coming from the bees belongs here. I don't think the person who edited this memory was the same person that encoded the data on to the bees. I think . . . I think YOU did it, Peter.>

<Me?>

<Yep.> Ashley was suddenly right beside me. <I think

that a part of you wanted to hold on to the truth of this scene, and that you hid that conversation in the nearest data store, which just so happened to be the bees. Even though you were only eight years old you managed to preserve that piece of data. I doubt if you even did it consciously.>

<You're saying that I have *hidden* the true memory *within* a faked memory?> I ask incredulously. <And I did it when I was eight?>

<Well.> Alpha says. <I knew there was something special about you.>

It makes me smile. Makes it sound less like craziness, too, somehow.

<If someone went to all the trouble of altering this memory . . .> Alpha says. <Then they must have a pretty good reason, don't you think?>

<There can only be one 'someone'.> I say grimly. <My father. He couldn't even leave me with a pure memory of my mother. What do I do?>

Ashley says: <Look around. Find the places that you might have hidden clues. And look out for any other

mistakes made in the editing process. Either way we might get some more detail.>

I get down on my hands and knees and I scan the area. The garden of that lost summer's day. Flowers and bees and grass.

There's nothing here.

Nothing except the questions I've got running around inside my head.

<Run the memory on a bit,> Alpha says. <Keep looking for anything that doesn't seem . . . quite right.>

I do exactly what she says.

I feel myself smile.

She is my world, I think, and it makes me feel warm.

And then I notice something.

My mother is not smiling.

She's standing there, looking down at me, her edges blurred by the brightness of the sun, and her face looks . . . sad. As if she is on the edge of tears.

I stop the memory again.

I look at my mother's edges, blurred by the brightness of the sun.

And I think about finding the edit marks around her image and how obvious they looked when they were pointed out to me. I think that the dazzling aura that surrounds her must have made it easier to edit the image, and that maybe the person doing the editing might have just slipped up, figured that the brightness would do a lot of their work for them, by masking the edges.

Maybe there is an answer in that aura.

I move closer and study the light around her. There are no longer any of the crude editing marks around her edges. I imagine a control panel and it appears in my hand as a controller. I locate a zoom and use it to enlarge a section of the aura. And I can see *something* in the midst of the light. I use my tools to alter the image, trying different filters.

<Good.> Ashley says. <There's definitely something there.>

It looks like the surface of some pretty rusty metal — which seems to prove that the background this memory originally occupied certainly was not our garden — but metal is metal and there is nothing to help place it in the real world.

But the rusty texture that I have revealed — poorly masked around my mother's image — makes me certain that my father *has* made a mistake. I'm sure that he never expected me to subject this memory to this type of scrutiny.

We are missing something.

Something elementary.

I need help, so I decide to message Perry.

/Hey man./ I say.

?Where the hex are you? Perry answers, sounding perplexed. /You've never missed a day's schooling in your life, buddy boy./ ?And now, what? ?You playing hooky?

/Something came up./ I tell him. /Something I really can't get into now. But I need your help./

/Of course you do, Petey. And I want to help you. I really do. But first you have to tell me something./

/Go on./

?Is this to do with the mystery girl? ?Gee, you realise that she's probably trying to get at me through you? ?You know, date the friend first . . .?

?Er, Perry?

?Ah, hex, she's listening, isn't she? His voice sounds embarrassed. *?OK then, what do you need?*

/I was thinking about the tiger on the train./

?You're weird, you know that?

?I'm weird? /It was you who thought it was a real picture. I remember I was the one who told you it was a fake./

Another one of Perry's bizarre photos, the tiger on the train was a Link sensation a few months back. An anonymous picture showing a white tiger on board a slider, that had tapped into the gullibility of the LinkGazing masses, and had people believing it without really questioning it.

Perry had sent it to me and I had replied with . . . well, pretty much what I've just said. Perry had then examined the photo and managed to break it down into its component parts. The source of the tiger in the picture had been a zoo in China.

?Is this an I-told-you-so call? Perry says, grumpily.

/On the contrary, I want you to tell me how you managed to work out where the tiger was from./

/Ask me a hard one, Peter! The answer is geotagging, simple as./

Geotagging.

I really am a fool sometimes.

I tell Perry thanks and promise to explain later and then I cut off the conversation.

I have always used Diary Plus for my LinkDiary. It costs, sure, and a lot of people don't use it, but it automatically logs geographical information and encodes it into every entry in the Diary.

I check the geotag for the entry and it tells me that it was logged as:

Location = **outside\714-3256-6245**.

Which is a numeric way of saying it happened in the garden at my home. I don't need to look it up, the software's already done it for me:

LocationLookUp = **7256 Avalon, New Cambridge, UK**.

But I know that's not true, so I access the entry's code log and scan through code. There's a lot of stuff I don't understand, but I know what kind of tag I'm looking for and it doesn't take long to trace the history of the image.

And I see that the tag was altered:

\rewrite geotag

And I see what it was altered *from:*

Location = **outside\612-9841-1793**.

Again I don't need to look it up, because the software's there way ahead of me.

LocationLookUp = **Naylor farm silos, Millgrove, New Cambridge, UK**.

I hear both Ashley and Alpha gasp.

I think 'leave' and step out of the memory. I don't want to see any more.

I lost my mother at a place that appeared in the Straker Tapes. A place that still appeared on the map software I'm running. Map software that I snagged from my father's home network.

It turns out that my father had map software that shows places that no longer exist, that were supposed to have never existed, if you were to believe his words.

I open my mouth to speak, but I can't think of a single word to say.

-14-

File: *113/50/05/wtf*

Source: *LinkData\LinkDiary\Peter_Vincent\Personal*

<LinkDiary Running>

We sat there for a short while, at the table in the Strakerite café, and sorted it through in our heads.

I was thinking about connections.

It seems that we live our lives making them, or looking for them, even sometimes breaking them, but very rarely do we stop to think about how dependent we are upon them.

I think that the Link itself is born from nothing more than a pressing need for us to connect. It's part of an instinct to reach out and share information, no matter how trivial or dull, just so we can feel like we are a part of a group, a set, a community.

We need to feel like we belong.

The Link provides us with all the connections we need. So much so that we pretty much let it run our lives for us now.

It's how we make sense of the world. So we look for patterns and linkages, because without them the world is a senseless blur.

Never mind that most of the time we're linking up with people we'll never *actually* meet; sharing memories and secrets and updates with strangers just so we don't have to feel so alone in the world, just so we can connect, even if the connection doesn't really mean anything at all.

And then, just today, I discover that *everything* is connected anyway.

Three days ago I would never have read the Kyle Straker Tapes. I wouldn't even have *considered* it. Indeed I would probably have laughed in anyone's face who suggested it.

Yet in the space of forty-eight hours I discover that everything in my life is connected to that secret history, written so long ago.

My father investigated them.

My mother disappeared out of my life at a location mentioned in them.

My memories have been altered to conceal the connections, but in spite of that, suddenly they have all converged.

One moment in time, where all the sticky threads lead.

The Grabowitz ghosts.

Mr Del Rey and the other missing members of the committee that investigated the Straker Tapes.

Me. My mother.

Alpha. Ashley.

LinkCrawlers and recovering missing information from eight-year-old memories.

The Straker Tapes themselves.

The Naylor silos — where Annette Birnie finally learned to fit in, and it only cost her her humanity.

A million eyes, watching.

Threads in a web, spun by a single spider?

My father?

Sitting in the middle of the web, feeling it pull as we

struggle against our fate, only becoming more ensnared as a result of our actions.

I suddenly realised that anything I had discovered — about my mother and the silos and the next upgrade — must be things that my father already knew. And if he could scoop handfuls of LinkActivity and examine them, like I had seen him do at the Science Council, then *he knew that I knew*. That was what he had been trying to tell me earlier.

I didn't know what my father was up to, I couldn't see what he had been planning for . . . for, well, years . . . at least since my mother disappeared. I just knew that he was doing *something*.

-15-

File: *113/50/05/wtf/Continued*

Source: *LinkData\LinkDiary\Peter_Vincent\Personal*

<LinkDiary Running>

Finally Ashley broke the silence.

'So it's true,' she said in breathless wonderment. 'All of it. Kyle Straker. Millgrove. Alien upgrades. The 0.4. And the silos . . . they still exist.'

Her voice was a mixture of wonder and horror.

I just nodded, feeling cold and scared.

'Do you know what this *means*?' Ashley said, her face suddenly pale and tense. 'We have proof, at last. Proof of all of it.'

'But we're running out of time,' I told her. 'There's another upgrade coming and I think it's happening today.'

'What are you talking about?'

So I told her about Alpha's father and the Committee for the Scientific Investigation of the Straker Tapes. I told her about the Grabowitz pictures and the young man counting down on his fingers.

Ashley looked disbelieving, about to laugh, but something in our faces stopped her. Her eyes narrowed into slits as she processed the information, and then her face came alive with the significance of what we were discussing.

'I have to tell someone,' Ashley said. 'I have to tell *everyone*.'

Alpha looked at me, and her eyes looked haunted by the sheer weight of the things we were finding out. 'And we have to go to Millgrove,' she said with absolute certainty. 'The geotag gave us the exact geographical location of the silos. That's where we have to go.'

'Why?' Ashley asked. 'What can you hope to achieve by going there?'

I gave Alpha a weak smile. She was right, of course.

There was nothing else that we could do.

'Answers,' I said. 'Maybe a way to stop it happening again.'

Ashley looked at us like we were insane.

'Good luck with that,' she said. 'I . . . I have to go. I have to call some people . . . I've got to tell people.'

'Then that's what you must do,' Alpha said. 'Peter and I have our own path to follow.'

Ashley looked like she wanted to say more, maybe try to talk us out of it; but she only shrugged.

'I wish you luck,' she said. Then she stood up and left the café.

The LinkCrawler apparatus she left on the table.

I looked over at Alpha.

'You sure about this?' I asked her.

'I . . . No, I'm not sure,' Alpha said. 'I just don't see that there's anything else for us to try.'

'If nothing else there might be some answers,' I said. 'Let's go.'

Alpha reached across the table and took my hands in hers. 'I'm sorry, Peter,' she said. 'I got you into all of this . . .'

'I was already a part of it long before I met you,' I told her, and then did something that surprised even me. I lifted her hands to my mouth and kissed her fingers. 'You have just shown me the way I guess I was always going.'

'To the silos?'

'To the silos.'

We left the café in silence.

-16-

File: *113/50/05/wtf/Continued*

Source: *LinkData\LinkDiary\Peter_Vincent\Personal*

<LinkDiary Running>

I pulled up a map from the Link and entered the precise coordinates of the silos into a 'search' field. The software quickly located the place we were headed. Then I laughed.

'What's funny?' Alpha asked, so I shared the map with her, explained what it meant, and she laughed too.

When everything's connected, and runs along patterns etched beneath the surface, sometimes you can only laugh.

You see, it would have been easy for me to have just lost it then. According to the map, my father hadn't needed to alter my memory very much at all.

Because that very last memory of my mother, the one

I remembered as taking place in the garden of our house, hadn't been that far wrong.

It just hadn't been *in* the garden.

Same location: wrong elevation.

My mother had said her goodbyes to me *under* the garden.

That was where the Naylor silos now resided. Under the ground beneath my father's house and land.

I lived *over* Millgrove.

And I always have.

RECOVERED SECTORS/
File-set 3

'The World Beneath'

*Occasionally we catch a glimpse. And tell stories of
ghosts and monsters. They're what make dogs
bark at night, or a cat's hackles rise.*

Daniel Birnie

interlogue

File: *224/09/12fin*

Source: *LinkData\LinkDiary\Live\Peter_Vincent\Personal*

<RUN>

Final set of entries, final few seconds of this world of ours.

There is something in the air. Like a storm brewing. I can taste it in my throat, dull and coppery and unpleasant.

I don't know how this is all going to turn out.

Whether we did anything at all.

Here are the last entries I will ever make.

-1-

File: *113/50/05/wtf/Continued*
Source: *LinkData\LinkDiary\Peter_Vincent\Personal*

<LinkDiary Running>

Alpha and I rode a slider back to my house, and neither of us really felt much like talking.

You think the world is one way, and you believe it for your whole life, and then something happens and shows you that you were wrong; the ground you thought was solid is made of ice, and it's melting away beneath you.

You deal with it how you can. That's all any of us do.

It's what Kyle Straker and Lilly Dartington did.

It's what Alpha and I were doing.

As we crossed the city we both stared out of the window, hand in hand, watching as our world rushed past us, looking the same as it always had, but different somehow, too. We flashed each other thoughts, and talked a bit about our fears, but mostly we just watched the city.

I guess you only really start to *see* something — really, truly see it — when it is in jeopardy. I suddenly realised that it all could just end in an instant. That the world we were passing through could suddenly become another one, just because of a signal transmitted from the depths of space, and everything we knew, everything we were, could just *change*.

Whether it would be a better world was irrelevant, really.

It wouldn't be *ours*.

And Alpha and I wouldn't be *us*.

Not really.

Not any more.

After the upgrade, Kyle Straker's parents were no longer his parents. They might have looked the same, but they weren't. They had become something else. Something more like us, like Alpha and me, creatures that could network through fleshy wires in our hands, and that could communicate without speaking.

To Kyle they were monsters.

Just like we would be monsters to people who missed the next upgrade.

Do you know something?

I realised then that I actually liked being me.

I liked being the way that I am.

I wanted to hang on to me.

And if that meant going up against alien programmers, or worse, my father, then so be it.

I would do everything in my power to remain me, and to keep Alpha Alpha.

We reached our stop and left the slider.

-2-

File: *113/50/05/wtf/Continued*

Source: *LinkData\LinkDiary\Peter_Vincent\Personal*

<LinkDiary Running>

I had to log Alpha in as a guest so we could get through the security fence. She held on to my hand as the fence performed its checks, a few nervous seconds passed, and then we were through.

'Nice,' Alpha said, staring up the path at the house. 'So this is where you live, huh, Peter?'

I felt a jolt of guilty embarrassment, thinking about what she had said earlier about the crystal neighbourhoods being slums in all but name.

'You're not going to get all Kyle Straker on me and stop calling, are you?' I joked.

'There's a reference you wouldn't have known to make last week,' Alpha said, rolling her eyes. 'You've got to admit that hanging around with me is nothing if not educational.'

I gave her a smile, but then purpose filtered back in, and humour suddenly felt out of place so we consulted the GPS.

We made our way in silence to the precise spot indicated on the map and stood on the lawn, pretty much in the centre of the front expanse, looking at the ground and trying to figure out how the hex to get under it.

The garden was calm and tranquil and there was a hazy quality to the light that made the place seem unreal and unfamiliar.

I've heard about archaeologists finding the past in the ground, digging up remnants of that which went before, but I don't think I have ever stopped to think just what that meant. That societies have always built upon the past, new societies on top of older societies; that layers of history stretch down into the very earth itself, sleeping, awaiting discovery.

I really didn't think that digging was going to be our way in, though. My memory had been altered so that it looked like it took place in this garden, when it had actually taken place beneath it, and I doubted that we got down there through spadework.

But get down there we did. Somehow.

Alpha stood there, looking baffled. 'So what do we do now?' she asked.

'There must be an entrance somewhere.'

'But why?' Alpha said, frustrated. 'Why would there be?'

And that was a good question. A really good question. Why the hex would there be an entrance to an underground world in the garden of our house? It was stupid. Just plain stupid. Like something out of a Last Quest scenario, but not the kind of thing that happened in real life.

Unless . . .

Oh, no.

Unless . . .

I shook my head and realised what I fool I had been.

The answer was right in front of me, and had been all along. 'What if my father's research into the Straker Tapes didn't end with that committee?' I said. 'What if he's known about the silos all along, and it's why we live here? He might be the world's greatest critic of your beliefs in public, but in private he's looking like a devoted believer. Except with him it's not even belief. It's not faith. It's certainty. He was on that committee and he found out the truth. He even built us a house slap bang over the evidence. Alpha, my father *knows* that the Straker Tapes are true. That was the real finding of the committee. It's true. It's all true.'

My voice had been steadily rising in volume, until I was almost shouting by the end of it.

Alpha looked at me with narrowed eyes.

'But why?' she asked me. 'Why would he pretend like that? Why would he hide the only real evidence of what Strakerites have been saying for centuries? Why, Peter?'

'Because he's up to something,' I answered.

I broke off, feeling sick to my stomach.

I couldn't say what had just occurred to me.

I just couldn't.

Alpha, however, could. 'And your mother?' she asked.

I had tears in my eyes. 'And my mother,' I whispered. 'She didn't leave us. He did something. He took her away from me.'

'And my father?' Alpha said weakly.

I nodded.

'It's all connected,' I said. 'Everything. And my father . . . he must be behind it all.'

It was a startling and terrible thought, one that reached into the very heart of who I was, or who I *thought* I was.

I'm not naïve.

At least not much.

But I genuinely thought that my father was a decent man. Driven in his work, maybe; surly and often indifferent to me, of course; cruel and dismissive to people who didn't share his opinions, always; but I never suspected him of being utterly dishonest.

Now I was certain of it.

Weird how your life changes, isn't it?

Well I had to do something, and standing in the garden was getting us nowhere, so I reckoned that there had to be a clue in the house, somewhere.

A secret door in his lab – and maybe that was why he'd never let me in there – or a hatch in the floor?

I was about to tell Alpha about my father's lab-at-home when she let out a sudden shriek and started flapping at her neck with panicked hands.

'Something just bit me,' she said indignantly. 'Right on the hexing neck.'

I hurried over to her and she stopped flapping, so I looked at where her fingers were now busy rubbing at a red patch on her skin.

'Let me look,' I said, and she moved her fingers aside, drawing back her hair so I could see clearly.

An angry red bump stood up from the surface of her skin, with a red pinprick at its summit. I thought that the red spot looked like a drop of her blood.

'That's weird.' I said. 'Maybe it is a bite. Or a sting.'

I put my finger on to the bump and it felt hot and inflamed. Alpha grunted in discomfort and I was just about to say sorry when I felt a sudden, sharp pain on the back of my hand.

I looked at it and for a second I thought that someone was playing a practical joke. There was an artificial bee sitting there, in the spot where I'd just felt pain: four centimetres long and glinting in the light of the sun.

It was just so strange. I mean the bees, they don't interact with humans at all. They're programmed not to.

They're programmed to stay away from us.

This one didn't seem to know that.

In fact, it had just stung me.

I tried to shake it off, but it was clinging on tight, so I had to swat it free with the other hand.

'Are you all right?' Alpha asked me.

'No,' I said. 'I just got stung. By a bee.'

'A bee?' Alpha said.

'A bee,' I repeated. 'One of my father's robot bees just stung me on the hand.'

Alpha looked at my hand, and at the twin of the bump she had on her neck, and her brow creased up.

'It must be the same one that stung me. It has to be a malfunction, or something.'

'Artificial bees don't have stings,' I said. 'Why would they? They don't need defence mechanisms, they're made of metal.'

'Well, this one did. Weird.'

'Weird indeed, I mean I have never heard of someone being stung by a bee before, and here we are, two in a minute . . .'

I broke off. Alpha was looking around and seemed a little freaked out.

'What?'

'Ssshhhhh,' she said, waving me quiet with her hand. 'Listen.'

I shut up and did as she instructed.

The garden was still and quiet, interrupted only by the buzz of bees.

The buzz of bees.

Not the quiet, languid hum of bees as they went from flower to flower, spreading pollen and ensuring the plants' reproduction though fertilisation; but rather a loud, disquieting buzz that sounded . . . *angry*.

Enraged.

'I don't like this,' Alpha said, and her voice was scared. 'Not one bit.'

'Me neither. Let's get inside. Quickly,' I said, gesturing at the house.

My hand froze in mid-air.

Off to our right, the air was suddenly becoming obscured by a dark, hazy disturbance. It took a second or two to make sense, but when it did I felt my growing disquiet graduating into full-fledged terror.

A huge cloud of bees was rising slowly from the bushes and flowers; a dense swarm that had to be made up of literally thousands of the artificial insects.

Rising up as if they had been hiding the whole time, waiting, and now the wait was over. The swarm looked like it had locked on to us, with the bee that had stung us both merely an advance scout for this terrible army.

We didn't have long.

I knew how fast these things could travel. I knew that the bees were capable of vertical take-off, and that they could move three times as fast as the creature they were modelled after.

What's the point in copying life, my father had once said, *if you don't take a little time to improve upon the original?*

Well, were there any more tricks he'd added?

'RUN!' I shouted.

We broke for the house just as the swarm surged forward. Thousands of bees, armed with stings, moving as one unit.

With us as their targets.

We ran.

Ran as fast as our legs could carry us, across the lawn, with that hideous buzz driving us onwards.

Five metres from the door, the swarm caught up with us. The air grew thick and dark and sharp and impossibly noisy. Metal bodies pinged off my face as I smashed into them, and I felt stings plunging into my flesh all over my body. I squeezed my eyes into barely open slits and focused on the front door ahead of me. Ignoring the stings, the pain, the incessant buzzing, I just aimed myself at reaching the rectangle that had suddenly become the only thought in my head.

Alpha was screaming but she didn't let it slow her down. We hit the front step at the same time and I already had my filaments ready to open the door. I don't remember deploying them, it must have been done with pure instinct.

I grabbed hold of Alpha and literally threw us both through the door, retracting my filaments even as gravity took hold and pulled us both down.

We hit the floor of the hall hard and lay there for a few seconds, with our limbs tangled up together, and I could only just hear the sound of the door mechanism closing over the roaring buzz of our pursuers.

My body was covered in stings that all screamed out in various shades of pain, but I managed to ignore them and even raised my head to watch as the door swung closed.

A small part of the swarm had already made it through into the house before the door finished closing. They were in the air above us, a sparse but no less deadly cloud of them, and they kind of hovered there as if they had temporarily lost sight of their targets.

The only way to get ourselves safe was simply to keep moving. I dragged myself along the floor on my knees and one hand, while the other grabbed a handful of Alpha's clothes so I could pull her along behind me. Putting my weight on to the stings on my hand and legs just made them hurt more, but I couldn't stop.

I didn't head for the nearest door, the dining room, because I could see the door was closed. Instead I headed towards my room because I had, as always, left it ajar.

This is insane! My mind kept saying. *Bees? My father's bees? Really?*

We reached my room just as the remaining bees locked on to us and started heading our way. I could hear them getting closer and I urged Alpha to hurry up. We threw ourselves forward, and made the threshold with a second or so to spare. Alpha and I bundled into the room and I kicked out to slam the door behind us. There was a resounding crash as the swarm hit the door and then Alpha and I were rolling around, brushing at our clothes, just in case we'd imported any of the swarm into my room hidden in their folds.

We lay on my bedroom floor, out of breath, adrenaline levels spiking off the scale, scared beyond our ability to speak, and for a short while the world ceased to make any sense.

My body was on fire in dozens of separate places, the most painful of which was a sting to my left eyelid that had swollen up and was rubbing against the eyeball.

I opened my eyes.

Alpha was hugging herself with arms that were trembling, and she was crying too. I crawled over to her and laid a hand upon her arm. She tensed away from my touch as if retreating from a threat.

Outside the bedroom door the swarm still buzzed, and I could hear the impacts as tiny bodies crashed into it, as if they were trying to get through to us.

Finally Alpha spoke.

'I guess . . . your father . . . doesn't want us to find out what he's up to,' she said in a voice that sounded somehow as if it had lost some of its clarity, some of its confidence.

'It's going to take a bit more than a few bees to stop us,' I said, full of false bravado.

'Do you know how many of those bees there are in the world?' Alpha asked, still sounding defeated. 'Billions. There are *billions* of them. And your father controls them all.'

'Looks like Tom Greatorex underestimated,' I said, feeling sick at the thought that had just occurred to me. Alpha looked at me blankly. 'He said there were a million eyes watching him, all the time . . .' I explained. 'What if he was talking about the *bees*? Tiny little spies that no one pays attention to?'

'What have we got ourselves into?' Alpha said, horrified. She looked at me and I saw three livid stings on her face — one on the cheek just below her right eye, one on the side of

258

her nose and one on her chin — and it suddenly flipped my mood from confusion to anger.

My father had no right to do this to us.

Any of it.

Alpha's father, my own mother, the bees, the lies, the secret machinations.

Whatever he was up to, I was going to stop him.

Or die trying.

-3-

File: *113/50/05/wtf/Continued*

Source: *LinkData\LinkDiary\Peter_Vincent\Personal*

<LinkDiary Running>

First, though, we were going to have to get out of my room.

Again, I thought of Kyle Straker and the moment he tried to escape from his own bedroom. I looked over to my window.

My heart sank.

The plexiglass was thick with the bodies of my father's bees, clambering over each other, urgently trying to get in. I wasn't even sure it would hold them.

Epic fail there, then. Door or window: both were out of the question.

And that left . . . nothing.

We were trapped.

I almost gave in to despair. It would have been so easy. But when I looked at Alpha I saw an expression on her face that pulled me back from the brink.

I'd been expecting to see fear, or pain, or resignation, but I got something else entirely: *expectation*.

A look that said: *so, what are we going to do now?*

And that also said: *I know you'll sort it out.*

And the spark of an idea came to me almost immediately.

I stood up and searched my room for something to help. Ideally I needed a sheet of metal, but I thought the chances of finding one of them was slim to none. Alpha watched on with a puzzled look, but didn't interrupt with unnecessary questions.

In my drawer I found a clothing blank: a neutral garment ready to have a style and a material type flashed on to it.

They're pretty much all that I wear these days. People can still buy clothes, but it seems a bit outdated and unnecessary. I just use my LinkHangers app, and I have any garment I need.

Any garment I need . . .

I sat down on my bed and thought about it.

261

A clothing blank had the potential to become any material.

ANY material.

I needed metal.

I've worn metal before.

I accessed my LinkHangers and navigated to a small and slightly shameful hanger section filed away as 'CosPlay'.

CosPlay, or Costume Play.

I only have a couple of templates hanging there. Last Quest stuff, from when I was completely obsessed with the games, instead of the 'mildly obsessed' I am now.

See, there are Last Quest get-togethers called QuestCons, where people turn up and meet up with people that they know from online activities but have never met in the flesh. And the true Last Quest fans . . . well, they kind of dress up as their online characters.

I selected a chain-mail shirt from a hanger and connected my filaments to the clothing blank.

Result: a metal mesh shirt.

I looked up at Alpha.

She was gazing at the garment in my hands with something close to amazement.

I guess she didn't know about Cosplay, Last Quest, or a Beserker called Tempest who wore a similar garment.

'We need a bee,' I told her.

-4-

File: *113/50/05/wtf/Continued*

Source: *LinkData\LinkDiary\Peter_Vincent\Personal*

<LinkDiary Running>

My father's bees used micro-electronics and some pretty amazing nano-engineering to give them the illusion of life. But they were, when all was said and done, machines. At their heart was a power cell, rechargeable of course, but it was not infallible.

Lightning could take them out in vast numbers.

It wasn't a problem — the factories that manufactured them could turn them out in batches of millions — and I'd even heard my father confessing that it wasn't cost-effective to make them hardier against electrical storms; lightning was actually a cash *generator*.

Bees that stop functioning need replacing.

My father's factories were only too happy to supply the replacements. At the usual price.

I'd got to thinking that storm clouds weren't the only things capable of generating bursts of electricity.

Anyone who's ever played BubblePop Evolved knows that.

However, instead of inanely popping soap bubbles, I was going to have a go at popping a bee.

Alpha stood by the door holding a glass, which I'd just used to take a legendary dose of calcium supplements. I had one hand on the door handle and my shoulder pressed against the door.

'Ready?' I asked, and Alpha was so tense and focused that she only managed a curt nod in reply.

I opened the door a crack.

Two bees made it into the room through the crack almost immediately and I slammed the door shut. By the time I'd finished, Alpha was standing with the glass pressed against the wall. The two bees were trapped within.

'Nicely done,' I said, and gathered up the mesh shirt. I connected to each arm of the garment with filaments from each hand and then put the shirt on the wall, next to the glass.

'Do it,' I said.

Alpha manoeuvred the glass along the wall, and then on to the shirt. The bees buzzed angrily against the glass but remained trapped.

'Here goes nothing,' I said, and thought about sending an electric charge from my body into the garment, but not the little charge that could pop a soap bubble; I thought much much bigger.

I felt a sharp, tearing pain in my spine and then through all the bones of my body as the electrical energy used up calcium at an alarming rate.

I felt the current discharge along my filaments and out along the metal mesh.

Nothing happened.

Oh, well, I thought, *it was a stupid idea anyway.*

The pain was levelling out into a dull throb of heaviness through my body.

So, we were well and truly trapped, then. I had been thinking that the charge would have been enough to knock the bees out of their flight at least.

Suddenly, one of the bees stopped flying about inside the glass and came to rest upon the mesh.

A blue spark leapt from the mesh to the bee and I could smell something like burnt ozone. The bee kind of bumped up off the mesh for an instant and, when it hit it again, it was dead.

Switched off.

Blown.

Alpha let out a whoop of triumph.

Me, I just breathed a huge sigh of relief.

Then we watched as the other bee found its way on to the mesh and suffered the same fate as its cellmate.

I shut off the current. Alpha took the glass away from the wall and the bees fell to the floor.

She grinned, poking at them with the toe of her shoe.

'When this is over you're going to tell me why exactly you have a chain-mail vest,' she said.

'Maybe,' I said, smiling. 'We'll see.'

I held the vest up.

'Wanna try it for real?' I asked her.

'Let's go,' she said, and kissed me on the cheek.

-5-

File: *113/50/05/wtf/Continued*

Source: *LinkData\LinkDiary\Peter_Vincent\Personal*

<LinkDiary Running>

This time Alpha dealt with the door, while I held the mesh up in front of me like a shield. I turned the current back on, and on a three count she threw open the door and then fell in behind me.

I moved forward towards the swarm.

The bees came straight at me, going directly for my face.

They hit the mesh and I stepped up the current even more, just to make sure.

I felt a surge of panic, that was still a HEX OF A LOT of bees, but then they started falling out of the air, and it was relatively easy to move the mesh around taking out any that I'd missed.

It was over in seconds.

It was almost an anticlimax if I'm honest.

'Wow,' was all Alpha could manage, a single word more than me.

We stepped over the fallen bodies of the slain bees and I disconnected from the mesh, bunched it up in my hand and made my way down the hall, Alpha following closely behind.

My father's study was unlocked and we went in. For the first time ever I noticed how empty the room was. A desk and a chair and a single picture on the wall that had always been his sole concession to stamping his personality on the place. He spent so much of his home time in here, thinking and working, but you would have been forgiven for thinking that the room was never used.

The picture was of a weird dome-like structure and I'd asked my father about it once.

'It's called a geodesic dome,' he had said, mildly irritated by the question. 'A beautiful construction that provides remarkable strength for its weight.'

I'd always thought that it was an odd picture for him to have on his wall, but then that's my father for you.

On the wall behind my father's desk was a door. The entrance to his laboratory.

I nodded towards the door and we made our way across the study and stood in front of it.

'This must be the way,' I said.

'You have a room in your house that you've never even been in?' Alpha said, in wonderment. 'You rich people are weird, you know that?'

'I know,' I said, and touched the metal plate that served as a locking mechanism.

Nothing.

I pushed at it.

Still nothing.

I put two hands on it and gave it a good hard shove.

More nothing.

I deployed filaments. When they touched the plate the door slid open. It didn't even seem to have any personalised coding to it. Anyone could have opened it, I reckoned.

What did that say about my father?

Was he incredibly trusting?

Or arrogant?

I stepped over the threshold.

It was dark inside.

Dark and cold.

And something else.

Moist . . .

I turned on my bioluminescence, and felt the usual tingle pass down my spine as I lit up the air around me. The dull red light was sufficient to show us that we were entering a tiny anteroom, with a platform that looked a lot like the *auto da fé* from Ellery Towers.

Alpha and I looked at each other, then stepped on to the platform.

It gave a high-pitched *beep* and then started to descend slowly.

-6-

File: *113/50/05/wtf/Continued*

Source: *LinkData\LinkDiary\Peter_Vincent\Personal*

<LinkDiary Running>

The platform took us on a slow climb down a narrow shaft. Alpha clung on to my arm as we descended, and I was only too happy for her to do it. I felt a tension that could easily grow into fear, and Alpha's closeness gave me some comfort.

After about twenty metres, we reached the bottom. The platform lurched, then steadied, and we stepped off into another small anteroom. It was even colder down here, and the air felt damp and unpleasant.

There was a reinforced metal door in front of us and, as we approached it, there was a loud noise as a mechanism inside ground and crashed, and then the door moved aside and there was bright light within.

We emerged, blinking, into a vast metal dome that stretched as far forward as the eye could see, and there were lighting rigs in bands across the ceiling high above us. My bioluminescence was unnecessary, and I killed it.

'Oh, my,' Alpha said. Which was two whole words more than I could manage. We moved forward, hardly able to believe the evidence of our senses.

The dome itself was an impressive feat of structural engineering, and the fact that it was hidden beneath the ground under part of the city was bizarre . . . but what it contained was truly mind-blowing.

It was an ancient, but perfectly preserved, village.

On all sides of us were buildings of a type that simply no longer existed in the world: squat little houses made of brick and wood and glass, none of them over three storeys high. They were like even older versions of the café that Alpha had taken me to earlier, and I had no doubt at all in my mind that I was walking along the streets of the village of Millgrove.

The light from above revealed every detail with almost

alarming clarity: an old-fashioned pavement; a weed-choked road.

We walked along, wide-eyed, and after a while Alpha pointed at something excitedly. A sign on the wall identified it as the Happy Shopper.

'It's smaller than I thought it would be,' she said, her voice over-brimming with excitement. 'Will you just look at that! It's real!'

I gave her a tight-lipped smile in reply. For her this was the confirmation of a lifetime of belief, and I could imagine that it must be intoxicating to finally discover proof as undeniable as this.

To me it had somewhat the opposite effect.

This place was proof that my father had been lying to me all of my life.

That he had been lying to the world.

That he had painted Strakerites as superstitious fools, while building a house above their most sacred place – Millgrove.

I felt sick and angry and betrayed.

Alpha was trying the door of the Happy Shopper, only to

discover that it steadfastly resisted her efforts.

'It's been *sealed shut*,' she said. 'There's some kind of transparent skin around the whole building.' She moved on further down the road. 'It's around all of the buildings. This must be why they are so perfectly preserved after all this time. It's like . . . it's like it's been kept as a museum . . .'

'Or a shrine,' I said, feeling the word fit better, somehow.

If Alpha heard, then she ignored me.

'If this is the Happy Shopper,' she was saying, 'then . . . then just down the road should be . . .'

She hurried down the road and I followed, my steps feeling heavy.

-7-

File: *113/50/05/wtf/Continued*

Source: *LinkData\LinkDiary\Peter_Vincent\Personal*

<LinkDiary Running>

Two minutes later I was standing on Millgrove's village green, with recently cut grass beneath my feet and stretching out all around me. It boggled the mind that this place was actually tended: that the grass was cut and the buildings were preserved. This place clearly meant something to my father, but there was no way that he kept this place maintained by himself.

That meant there must be other people who knew that Millgrove was down here, under the streets of New Cambridge; but no one had shared that knowledge with the Strakerites, who must have dreamed of finding the place mentioned by their prophet.

I couldn't work it out.

Why? Why would my father go to all this trouble? Why would he keep the mythical village clean and tidy and preserved in a plastic skin?

I watched as Alpha examined the bus shelter that squatted by the side of the green, and then as she ran on to the grass, laughing with pleasure.

'The Millgrove talent show,' she yelled. 'Mr Peterson and his ventriloquist act. It happened here. All of it. Peter, LOOK!'

She span around on the spot with her arms fully extended. 'Thank you.' She came over and whispered in my ear. 'I never thought . . .'

It was all too much for her, I guess, for she couldn't articulate the thought.

We stayed there for a short while, under the artificial suns of the dome's lighting system, and then Alpha sighed and we moved apart. She started looking past the green, up the road that snaked by, and out of the village.

'Do you think that THEY are still there?' she said, and her tone was an odd mix of awe and terror.

'The silos?' I asked her. 'That's got to be the Crowley road,' I pointed at the street that led out of the village, 'so the Naylor farm should be up there somewhere.'

I consulted the GPS map and it confirmed what we already knew in our hearts.

'We should go there,' Alpha said. 'I think it's where we'll find the answers.'

'And maybe the man who knows them all,' I said. 'And has known them all along.'

Alpha gave me a sad look. 'This must be hard for you. I've turned your world upside down, haven't I?'

I shook my head.

'No, Alpha,' I told her, seriously. 'I think you might just have put it the right way up.'

She studied my face for a couple of seconds, and then nodded.

'Lead on,' she said.

-8-

File: *113/50/05/wtf/Continued*

Source: *LinkData\LinkDiary\Peter_Vincent\Personal*

<LinkDiary Running>

The same care and attention that had been afforded Millgrove did not, it seemed, extend to the countryside outside the village. This should have been open fields, but it was all overgrown and chaotic, and looked like it was being claimed back by nature.

The road, however, was beautifully preserved and it looked so strange cutting through the tangled brambles and weeds that filled the land on either side.

We picked our way along, and soon we spotted the towers that meant we were approaching our destination.

A part of me wasn't *that* happy to see to them.

They might hold answers to the questions that consumed us — that consumed me — but there was a grim inevitability about them that made me feel uneasy and scared.

And, of course, there was the other thing.

I had seen them before.

I realised it the moment I saw them. It was like an enormous flash of déjà vu that stopped me in my tracks.

I was just rationalising it away, thinking that of course I would recognise them if this was *really* where the farewell scene with my mother had played out, when the darkest thought of the day rose up and blotted out everything.

Because suddenly I remembered *exactly* where I had seen them before.

I didn't even have to think back very far.

Just as far as that weird, disturbing dream I'd had. When the crystal towers suddenly sheared and changed, these were the concrete structures they had become.

A friendly tap on the arm from Alpha pulled me out of it, but a feeling of dread — like a lead weight in my stomach — persisted as we moved closer to the silos.

The dome was narrower here — no longer a dome at all

really, but something more like a high-ceilinged tunnel – and I could see that the countryside ended prematurely on either side, and the tunnel wall could be seen in the distance.

A path had been cleared though the brambles and weeds, leading to the Naylor farm and then the two towers that loomed above us, looking sinister and oppressive.

The closer we got, the bigger they appeared.

I thought of Kyle and Lilly, about Annette Birnie and the strange, moving language that enveloped her, turning her into one of them . . .

Or should that be 'one of us'? I corrected myself, and didn't like the way the thought made me feel.

We rounded a bend and then both of us stopped and stared ahead of us, uncomprehending.

The silos stood, tall and silent, but they weren't the only things there.

Someone's been busy down here, I thought.

A number of large holes had been bored into the sides of the towers, with bunches of wires and cables coming out and being fed down into banks of computer machinery. The machines themselves were sunk down in a vast circle, accessible by four metal ladders at compass points around the edge of the crater.

The machines were all linked together with more cabling, and I could see that a number of tunnels led off from the rim of the crater like spokes on some gigantic wheel. Cabling ran from the crater down the throat of each tunnel.

A couple of white-coated technicians were working down there, attending to the machines, and they were making adjustments and programming data into old-fashioned keyboards on the front of each terminal. Alpha looked shocked to see them there, but I just gave her a shrug. I guess I was running short of the ability to be surprised.

The air felt different here. It was still cold, but the dampness had gone, and had been replaced by a weird kind of static charge that, although it was far from hot, made my skin feel so agitated that I was beginning to sweat.

The hairs on my neck were bristling, too.

Alpha was pointing at something and I followed her finger to a huge computer display that was part of the wall that split off into tunnels. It was showing numbers a metre high that were steadily counting down: 53.23, 53.22, 53.21, 53.20 . . .

In the areas in front of the clock, the banks of computers were arranged in concentric circles, and more cables led from each bank and into a metal and frosted glass dome made up of triangles that sat at the very centre of the man-made crater.

I recognised the shape.

It was the same geodesic design that my father had on his study wall; the only picture that had ever been there.

Alpha was still staring, transfixed by the countdown on the screen – 53.15, 53.14, 53.13 – and I put my hand on her shoulder.

'You know that it's counting down to the next upgrade, don't you?' she said, looking back at me. 'We've got less than an hour until the world changes. Forever. Again.'

She was only saying what I already knew in my heart, but hearing the words spoken made it seem all the more true, all the more terrifying.

Words gave concepts power.

Once they were released, there was no choice but to understand them, no matter how painful they might be.

I'd known that time was counting down. I'd known it

since I realised that young man in the Grabowitz photos was showing us the time we had left on his fingers. I'd known what it meant for all of us, but it wasn't until I saw that clock, and heard Alpha's words that I *truly* understood our situation.

My father was able to predict the time of the next upgrade. He'd put wires and cables into the silos and was processing the code within, all so he could . . . *so he could what?*

What was to be gained by knowing the precise time of the next transmission from the alien programmers that Kyle Straker talked about?

What could my father possibly hope to *gain*?

Even though it felt like the last thing in the world I wanted to do, I knew I had to get inside the geodesic dome. It was the only thing there was left to us: we had to find my father.

-9-

File: *113/50/05/wtf/Continued*

Source: *LinkData\LinkDiary\Peter_Vincent\Personal*

<LinkDiary Running>

Down further into the pit.

That was how it felt.

Like I was descending into one of the dark places of some strange, primitive myth, where souls burned in eternal torment for deeds performed in life.

There's a reason we keep building upwards, you know: an instinctive need — somewhere in our race memory — to climb away from the dark spaces that lurk beneath the skin of our world.

As I climbed down the ladder into the crater I wondered what kind of person went against that primal programming;

what kind of man my father was.

And here I was, following him down. Not quite what I expected the phrase 'following in his footsteps' to mean.

I'd like to think that I was trying to help out Alpha, and maybe try to stop the whole of humanity being upgraded again by those . . . beings that saw us as nothing more than organic computers that they could reprogramme whenever they got some weird cosmic urge.

I'd like to think my motives were good and noble and true, but I wonder if maybe I just wanted to confront my father with the things I knew, that I wanted to face up to him, then to make him tell me what he did to my mother.

Maybe it was a combination of both, I don't know.

In the end, I guess, it doesn't really matter.

The metal of the ladder's guard rails vibrated as I lowered myself down, a deep rumble that pretty soon started to make my hand ache. I ignored it, finished the descent, and stepped off on to the floor of the crater. When I was clear, Alpha jumped down the last few steps.

'What now?' she asked, her face flushed.

I shrugged. 'I'm making it up as I go along,' I told her,

and then pointed to the geodesic dome at the centre of everything. 'But there looks as good a place as any to start.'

We used the backs of the computer banks as cover and headed into the centre of the labyrinth.

-10-

File: *113/50/05/wtf/Continued*

Source: *LinkData\LinkDiary\Peter_Vincent\Personal*

<LinkDiary Running>

I realised that my connection to the Link was down when I tried to flash Alpha a warning about a technician who had suddenly left his workstation and was heading our way. He hadn't seen us yet, but we were going to be in his eye line pretty soon.

Alpha was following a metre or so behind me, so I thought: */Alpha. Down./* But there wasn't the usual sensation of the Link behind the attempt at a message. I tried again, and again there was nothing, as if the mechanism for transmissions had suddenly disappeared.

I might not wholly trust the Link, but it was a genuine shock to find it was no longer there when I needed it.

In the end I just waved at her, and gestured for her to get down. We both fell into crouches behind a computer, and the technician went by without even looking our way. He latched on to another computer and started punching keys. It was a case of modern technology meeting old: the only place you see keyboards these days are in museums.

Alpha caught up to me.

'Can you access the Link?' I asked her, and she spent a few seconds trying before shaking her head.

'Must be something here jamming it,' she said, then added: *'We were in the middle of a mobile phone dead spot.'*

I realised she was quoting from the Straker Tapes.

'Pretty weird, isn't it?' I asked.

She shrugged. 'Show me something today that isn't.'

We went another couple of banks down, then I peered around the edge, saw that we were unobserved, and hurried across towards the dome in the centre.

We circled around it, looking for a way in. Cables and wires went into the dome through un-glassed areas, but there didn't seem to be anything as useful as a door on the whole structure.

We completed a full circuit of the dome and there simply was no entrance.

'Now what?' Alpha asked.

'Scout around,' I said. 'Look for something we can use to smash our way in.'

'We're going to draw attention to ourselves.'

'I'm counting on it.'

A quick recon of the area turned up a few loose tools, all too small to be of any use, and two lengths of metal piping. One was about fifteen centimetres long, but the other was a metre long and pretty heavy. I hefted it in my hand and nodded.

'This should do it,' I said, and then strode over to the dome, raised the pipe up, and smashed it into one of the glass panels. The pipe just bounced off it, doing no damage, and the vibrations sent the pipe spinning out of my hand.

The sound was loud and jarring and everyone in the area must have heard it.

Alpha was giving me a 'What was that supposed to be?' look, and I was about to explain that it wasn't glass and all I'd done was hurt my hand, when a section of the dome suddenly unhinged and flipped open.

So that's how it was done.

Seconds later my father emerged from within. If he was surprised to see me then he did a very good job of hiding it. He ran a hand through his hair, fixed Alpha with a coolly appraising look, and then turned to me.

'Ah, Peter,' he said. 'Has no one ever told you that it's rude to enter people's property without being asked?'

I fixed him with my best steely look. 'Has no one ever told you that you're a liar and a hypocrite?' I countered, furious. 'And that sending swarms of your robot bees to kill your own son is evidence of pretty lousy parenting?'

He let out a single, measured, snort of laughter.

'The answer to your first question is: yes, frequently,' he said. 'And do you know what? I don't listen to them, either. While I salute your ingenuity and courage and even, to a certain extent, your wilful disobedience, this really isn't the time or the place to trade insults.

'Your second question, however, is fundamentally flawed. It presupposes knowledge of events of which I am entirely ignorant. It sounds like you fell foul of the security system I implemented to protect my own property. That they attacked you, and this is news to me, was purely accidental. It's more than likely a result of bringing an unauthorised guest along with you. As you will have noticed on your way in, I have things to protect.'

I thought that was probably as close to an apology as I was ever going to get from him: *It was an accident that a swarm of murderous robot bees almost killed you.*

'Now, much as this is a pleasant break in a very busy day,' he continued, 'I really must get back to work. We are perched on the cusp of the future, and I have things I must attend to. If we could pick this up later . . .?'

'Later?' I snorted. 'I think we both know there isn't going to be a *later*, don't we? I don't know what you're up to, but I think I deserve an explanation at least.'

'Do you now?' my father said, irritated. 'And what makes you think I owe you *anything*, my boy?'

'Oh, I don't know,' I said, 'Maybe because I'm your son? Or if that isn't reason enough, how about out of human decency? You know that the Straker Tapes are true, and you lied to keep it a secret; you've made their believers out to be idiots who are beneath society's contempt. I think I deserve to know why. I think we both deserve to know why.'

My father gave Alpha another look, wrinkled his nose and then shook his head.

'There really is no time. I must confess that I mis-calculated. I thought that you would spend your day with those contact lenses in your eyes, chasing ghosts, and leave me free to do what has to be done.'

The contact lenses.

His 'gift' to Alpha and me.

I'd forgotten all about them.

We'd looked at them, thought it was a weird sort of gift to give, and then they'd gone straight back in my pocket.

'You didn't even put them in, did you?' my father laughed. 'It really is true, about parents not knowing their children, isn't it? You were supposed to be consumed with curiosity. You were supposed to put them in your eyes, and then we wouldn't be having this conversation.'

He seemed genuinely stunned by his miscalculation.

'Tell you what,' he said, 'Why don't you pop them in now, see what you were missing?'

'We haven't got time for games,' I said. 'I want answers.'

'Then do as you are told,' my father said curtly. 'And I'll even stick around to explain.'

-11-

File: *113/50/05/wtf/Continued*

Source: *LinkData\LinkDiary\Peter_Vincent\Personal*

<LinkDiary Running>

So, with the future of the world we knew ticking down on the clock on the wall of the crater, I lifted two of the lenses from the case, and offered the other pair to Alpha.

We looked at them, not sure just how they were supposed to be used, until my father lost patience, took an identical case from his own pocket, took out a lens on his fingertip and proceeded to demonstrate how to place it over an open eye.

'Simple,' he said, as if explaining it to infants. 'Now you do it.'

I copied his actions, brought up my finger, steadied it

because it was shaking, and popped the lens in place on my right eyeball.

It stung as it made contact, and my eye started to water. I blinked a few times and felt it move, then settle, on the curve of my eye. It was a horrible sensation, and I really couldn't believe that people ever used to do this so they could see normally.

The left one was next, but I hesitated. I had a pretty nasty sting to that eyelid and I had to be more careful getting the second lens in place.

Soon I had two watering, stinging eyes and completely blurred vision.

'You have to wait a few seconds,' my father said. 'The circuitry inside each lens has to connect to your optic nerve.'

Already my vision was resolving out of the murk.

Then, suddenly, it was clear.

If it wasn't for the slight alien pressure on my eyes, I guess I wouldn't have known I was wearing them.

I looked around, wondering what I was supposed to be seeing with the lenses in place, but they had no effect on me at all. I looked at Alpha and she looked at me.

She shook her head.

Nothing.

'These are great and everything . . .' I started, but my father cut me short.

'You actually have to be looking in the right place,' he said, sounding like he thought I was about five years old. 'If you turn your attention up a level, to the silos, I think you'll see what I mean.'

He pointed as he spoke and Alpha and I followed it to the place he was indicating with his finger.

'They're drawn to them,' he said. 'Goodness only knows why. I think they sense what's coming . . . I think they can always sense it . . .'

I stopped listening to him and stared.

At first there was nothing; just the silos. But then there was an odd feeling in my head, as if my brain had just . . . *clicked* . . . and there they were.

I could see them.

I could really see them.

Three shadowy figures stood next to one of the silos, staring up at it. There was a man, a woman and a child, where once there had been nothing.

I shuddered.

Ghosts, I thought, *I'm looking at ghosts*.

They had the same kind of look of *not-belonging* that the other people in the Grabowitz photos had possessed: an out-of-time look that was partly to do with the style of their clothing and partly to do with the fact that something about them just looked . . . *wrong*.

I thought about the Straker Tapes, and Mr Peterson saying how things from Earth follow visual rules, and I realised that he hadn't been entirely correct.

These people looked wrong, but it wasn't because they were from elsewhere. It was because I wasn't supposed to be seeing them.

The three figures were holding hands, and I couldn't take my eyes off them. They looked like that at any second they could just wink out of existence.

Ghosts.

A previous software version.

Only made visible by the lenses in my eyes.

I felt a tremendous surge of sorrow for them, and

suddenly the woman looked back over her shoulder, as if she had sensed that she was being observed.

Her eyes met mine.

For a moment I thought that we had just made some kind of contact, that the look we were sharing was profound and meaningful, but then she looked far past me, shook her head, and turned back to the silo.

And then I saw the others.

It was like a gate had been opened in my mind, only it was more like a floodgate because now . . . now there were more of them.

I could see maybe twenty-or-so other figures, standing around the base of the silo and staring up at it. Young and old, male and female, but all of them possessing that strange quality of not-belonging.

'The lenses correct the perceptual screening process,' my father was saying. 'They undo the programming that filters out the past versions of humanity.'

I looked over to Alpha and saw that she was watching the *other* people too.

I felt a hand on my shoulder and turned around. I was

shocked to find it was my father's hand.

'There is a secret human history,' he said, and there was something in his voice that sounded like regret, 'that runs a parallel course to our own. And it is a history of the lost.'

'The ones left behind,' I said. 'The 0.4.'

My father laughed, and removed his hand from my shoulder.

'Oh, Peter,' he said, and there was genuine disappointment in his voice. 'I had such high hopes for that brain of yours, but it stubbornly refuses to see through to the *heart* of things. The Straker Tapes were recorded a millennium ago; we've been upgraded many times since then.

'The silos are the key, you see, and the information they contain unlocks so many secrets for those brave enough to look.

'Brave enough and smart enough.' He said the last without a hint of self-consciousness, just as a plain statement of fact.

'It's breathtaking, really; the data that we have managed to extract from the Naylor silos. We have been able to tap into much of the history of our software upgrades, and to trace human development by the computer code that caused its changes.

'Did you know that an earlier upgrade, about five hundred years ago, actually produced humans without lips? It didn't last long – a decade, give or take – before it was reversed in a small update that also corrected a bug they were having with our dreaming states. But do you see what it means?

'We have always believed that our evolution was a one-way process of development, and that when we lose things we lose them forever. That there is no regaining lost abilities, lost attributes.

'Turns out that it's completely untrue,' he said, with something approaching glee. 'Tomorrow could see us with fins and gills.'

He switched from gleeful to solemn without missing a beat. 'Tomorrow,' he said. 'You both know what today is, don't you? It's why you're here.'

'It's the last day for humanity as we know it,' Alpha said, and her voice was raw and full of anger.

'And here's the thing,' my father said. 'If they can control our development, then they can always make sure that we are *less* than they are. By upgrading us they can *limit us.* Keep us their slaves. Forever.'

'And you've known about all of this, and kept it a secret, for how long? Years?'

I'm not sure what Alpha had been expecting my father to say, but she seemed genuinely derailed by what he *did* say.

'Decades,' my father answered. 'So you're the girl that's filling my son's 'Lilly' paradigm. How sweet.'

Alpha looked at him with wide eyes, and demanded: 'What does that even mean? What the hex is a Lilly paradigm?'

My father gave her a cryptic look.

'Why did Lilly Dartington put her hand up at the Millgrove talent show?' he asked her.

'No one knows,' Alpha answered quickly. 'We only ever find out Kyle's side of the events; Lilly's thoughts are never revealed.'

My father shook his head.

'The Straker Tapes weren't the only record of the events at Millgrove,' he said, and there was a triumphant note in his voice. 'Lilly left a diary, you know. Handwritten, if you can believe it. It takes up pretty much where Kyle's story left off, as if he had passed the baton on to her as chronicler of the new world.

'*The Travel Diary of Lilly Dartington* is, in many ways, a more fascinating text than the Straker transcriptions, because Lilly had an intellectual depth to her observations that is often missing in those of her boyfriend. She also details the mental struggle of being left behind, and describes encounters with some of the 1.0.'

'There is no such book,' Alpha said through gritted teeth.

My father smiled.

'Not seeing something is not a logical case for something not existing,' he said smugly. 'I've never seen gravity, but I know it exists.

'Lilly's diary is real. I should know. I own it. Anyway, in an early entry she recalls the moment that she volunteered to be a subject for Daniel Birnie's stage hypnotism. What is the Strakerite view on the subject of her motivations?'

'That it is unknowable,' Alpha said, and there was an edge to her voice.

My father didn't notice.

'You don't even while away the evenings in New Lincoln Heights by wondering?' he asked.

'No,' Alpha said. 'We don't. There is enough information in the tapes without us creating groundless interpretations.'

My father stroked his chin thoughtfully.

'Well let me clear up the mystery for you,' he said, 'using evidence from another contemporary source. Lilly saw Kyle's hand go up, and she was aware that his own experiences as a stand-up comedian made that a courageous thing for him to do. He was willing to risk embarrassment in front of his peers, just to save his friend from being embarrassed himself.

'Lilly couldn't bear to be a part of an audience that was laughing at Kyle. It took less than a second for her to run it through in her head and for her to reach her decision; indeed her hand was already rising before Kyle's hand made it fully up into the air.

'In that instant, she sided with Kyle against the majority. And against Simon, who was, nominally at least, her boyfriend at the time.

'Lilly later says in her diary that in that moment, when she chose to side with Kyle, she also chose her future path; that while Kyle blundered into being a 0.4 in a 1.0 world – with his attempt to save Danny from embarrassment – Lilly chose to follow him, and thus chose her path.

'And never once in her diary does she consider that the choice that she made was the wrong one.

'That is the Lilly paradigm.

'Peter was always going to be a Kyle, someone dragged into events beyond his understanding; I've known that since the day he was born.

'But you.' He shook his head. 'You are the proof of the Lilly paradigm. That someone always chooses to follow a Kyle into the fire, regardless of the consequences.'

I suddenly felt my scalp bristling. I could hear the voice of the strange man in my dream as he said: *She'll follow you into fire, but why would you lead her there?*

'I'm here because I'm looking for my father,' Alpha said. 'Not because of some invented paradigm.'

'Oh, really?' My father's eyes rolled back to whites and then he started speaking in a voice that wasn't quite his own.

'**File:** *113/47/04/cbt*

Source: *LinkData\LinkDiary\Amalfi_Del_Rey\Personal.*

"I can't sleep. I can't stop thinking about him; about Peter. There is something so tragic about the path he is walking, and I find myself running it over and over in my mind. I thought that he was helping me find my father, but now I am sure it is more than that. This sounds crazy, but I think I'm helping him, by making sure that he does not tread that path alone.""

My father's eyes rolled again, and the whites were no longer showing.

Alpha's face was taut, her jaw clenched, and her eyes looked like steel ball bearings.

'That is my *private diary*,' she snarled.

'*Was*, my dear girl,' he said. 'Those tenses can be a little tricky, can't they? It WAS your private diary, but then you traded link addresses with my son and I gained access to it and it stopped being private. My son has no secrets from me; he just thinks he has.

'Now I don't know if either of you will ever be truly satisfied with any answers I can give you, and time really is running out . . .'

He pointed to the countdown clock, which had reached

48.22.

'So if we could hurry this up, I really need to get back to work . . .'

'What work?' I said angrily. 'Fiddling while Rome burns?'

'Ah, the benefits of a proper education,' he said sarcastically. 'Seeing as you are asking, I am in the process of engineering a better tomorrow. A delicate operation that requires my full attention . . . well, about now.'

He walked back into the geodesic dome without another word.

After a few seconds Alpha and I followed him.

-12-

File: *113/50/05/wtf/Continued*

Source: *LinkData\LinkDiary\Peter_Vincent\Personal*

<LinkDiary Running>

Inside the dome it was almost unpleasantly warm and humid, and the air tasted bad. A small space was packed with racks of computer equipment of a type unfamiliar to me.

Bundles of grey cables and rainbow-coloured wires ran along nearly all of the available wall space, and they all fed into a large processing unit in the middle of the room, which then fed out into smaller units and a triptych of large display screens.

My father immediately started pushing buttons and tapping keys.

The central monitor of the three was filled with a

bizarre language of hooks and eyes and shifting characters. It looked like Kyle's description of the alien code on the screen of Mrs O'Donnell's computer, and later in the silos themselves.

It was no real surprise that it was also the exact same language I had seen infecting the city in my dream.

To the left was a screen that seemed to be translating the alien language into columns of what looked like binary code. To the right was a selection of animated readouts and dials, showing some kind of power grid.

Alpha touched my arm and pointed to a space between the central hub and the outer wall of the dome.

'Is that . . .?' she asked, breathlessly, and then I felt the same kind of switching feeling in my brain that I'd had seeing the people around the silos, and suddenly the contact lenses I was wearing pulled a shape out of the ether.

Another ghost, coming into focus.

Oh, this just wasn't fair.

This wasn't fair at all.

I had imagined this moment, played it over in my mind so many times, but not here, not like this.

The person resolving out of the murk — becoming visible as the perceptual filter concealing her was stripped away by the lenses' adjustments — was my mother.

-13-

File: *113/50/05/wtf/Continued*

Source: *LinkData\LinkDiary\Peter_Vincent\Personal*

<LinkDiary Running>

She was *almost* there, phasing half-in and half-out of the everyday world, and then the image sharpened, and she was standing in front of us.

My mother's lips were moving, but I couldn't hear anything she was saying.

It couldn't be.

It couldn't be *her*.

'Your mother just asked you a question.' My father's voice bled in over my internal chaos.

'Is there an ear thing so I can hear her?' I asked.

My father let out a dry chuckle and I saw that in the time

we had been inside the dome he had been busy attaching wires and electrodes to his own head, so that his skull was festooned with a squid-like arrangement of coloured wires.

It was another bizarre moment in a thoroughly bizarre day.

'There's no need,' he answered, attaching another skein of wires to himself. 'It's a perceptual filter, but its effect is already shifted and you are now aware of her. Just concentrate. I know it's difficult for you but . . .'

Any opportunity to criticise me. Still, I did what he said.

I concentrated on my mother's face, watching her lips move soundlessly, and I struggled to make her words audible.

At first there was nothing, but then I heard a voice phasing out of nowhere, like speech, but as if it was being heard underwater.

I focused on the sound, and it wasn't long before it became so clear that I couldn't understand how I hadn't heard it before.

'. . . to see you,' my mother was saying.

'Mum?' I asked, a bare whisper, my voice throttled with emotion.

She looked different than I remembered, but of course she did. That was seven years ago. There was grey in her hair, and her clothes looked ... well, *older* I guess.

My mother nodded.

'I have never been far away,' she said. 'I ... I had to ... stay close to you. I've watched you grow. It's so good to finally be able to talk to you.'

'Mum ... how ...?' I felt like I was eight years old again; as if the years that had passed in between our meetings had been a dream, and now I was finally waking up.

'It's all so complicated,' she said.

'Try,' I said, with a little more edge than I knew was there. 'Where did you go?'

'Nowhere. I've always been right here.'

'I don't understand.'

'The project required someone to ... downgrade, back to a previous software version. I insisted that that someone should be me. You father argued against it, but I am pretty stubborn when I need to be.'

'Downgrade?' I spoke the word and it ended up a question.

My mother nodded.

'Once we started studying the code that upgrades us, it wasn't long before it became possible for us to reverse the process. To send someone *back* to a previous software version. To travel into the kind of world that Kyle and Lilly describe in their accounts.

'We needed someone to make that sacrifice. I couldn't let anyone else do something I wasn't prepared to do myself. I argued, won . . .' A slight smile played across her lips. 'And I fell through the cracks.'

I couldn't believe what I was seeing, or what I was hearing. I was in a seething turmoil, and a flicker of anger boiled to the surface.

'You wanted this? You *left* me . . .' I said.

'I HAD to, Peter, you can see that, can't you? Everything we are doing here today hinged upon having someone who could report from . . . the other side of human existence. We didn't know then that it would be a one-way trip, but it was a risk we were willing to take. That I was willing take.'

'What are you talking about?' I asked desperately. 'What is this all about? I don't understand.'

'We are in the process of making things better,' my

mother said. 'For millennia we have continued along a path that is not our own. Our minds and bodies have been subject to the whims of our programmers. We no longer know what it even *means* to be 'human'; we're nothing more than a commodity that just so happens to be a race. All these thoughts and feelings, the majesty of human existence, the specific individual experience of simply *being alive*, they can all be taken from us in an instant.

'Peter, it isn't right. And it certainly isn't the way that things are supposed to be for us.'

'Leaving me wasn't right,' I said, and I felt Alpha squeezing my arm. 'I can't believe this. I always thought that it was something I'd done that made you leave, but this . . .' I gestured around me. 'I don't get it.'

My mother looked at me, and I realised that there was no kindness or love in the look. In that moment I knew that I had been wrong about her. I had thought that she was all the good things that my father lacked. All I saw in her eyes was a passionate intensity for this *project*. They were the eyes of a zealot.

'Well, I'm sorry that you think your precious childhood

315

was more important than the future of the human race,' she said coldly.

The mother that I'd clung to in my heart was a myth.

I felt sick.

'And my father?' Alpha suddenly demanded. 'What happened to him? And Leonard DeLancey, Edgar Nelson, Thomas Greatorex? Were they 'sacrifices' too?'

My mother glanced at Alpha for the first time, as if only just noticing her presence. The look she gave was both stern and dismissive.

'The findings of the Straker Committee could never be made public,' she said. 'But everyone involved with it was changed by the experience. Changed forever. Far from disproving a tiresome folk tale, the committee ended up confirming its reality.

'The other people you mention, the other members of the committee, they all agreed that silence was in our best interests, and they accepted their roles in what needed to be done: they have been downgraded too.

'All except for Tom.

'Yes, poor Tom. The responsibility never sat easily on

his shoulders, you know. Some things are just too big. Too important. It takes a special kind of person to do what needs to be done. Instead of fulfilling his sworn duty, Tom Greatorex chose to take his own life.

'The future does not belong to the weak. To the cowardly. It belongs to people of vision. Of courage. Of fortitude . . .'

'Nice sound bites,' I interrupted. 'But if it's true about Alpha's father, then I think she deserves to see him, don't you?'

'That's not possible,' my mother said. 'The Naylor farm silos are not the only focus point for the alien programming code. Iain – your father – he's acting as downgrade liaison to the Wiltshire site; Lenny DeLancey is heading up things in Egypt; Ed Nelson is involved in the Chinese project. Tom was to headline the European end of things, but as the time drew closer he started behaving erratically and became increasingly paranoid.

'Someone else is handling things there.'

'What, so you're really a band of global resistance fighters?' I asked mockingly.

'If that's how you want to look at it,' my mother responded, ignoring my sarcasm. 'We are simply no longer going to tolerate the interference of others in our evolutionary path.'

'And how, exactly, do you intend to stop them interfering?' Alpha asked.

My mother wrinkled her nose, then shrugged.

She pointed to the door of the dome.

'Follow me,' she said. 'I'll show you.'

-14-

File: *113/50/05/wtf/Continued*

Source: *LinkData\LinkDiary\Peter_Vincent\Personal*

<LinkDiary Running>

So we followed my mother's ghost across the crater, picking our way through the machinery and cabling, and into the mouth of one of the tunnels.

Earlier I had wondered about the number of people that maintained this place; now I found myself thinking about the amount of manpower that had gone into the creation of the whole complex.

How had this all stayed a secret?

How many people knew what was going on down here?

It seemed that my mother was casting herself in what my father would probably call the Danny Birnie paradigm – the one who would take it upon themselves to detail the brutal truths of our situation, and take pleasure from it.

I was tired of it all.

I didn't want to be here.

I'd come for answers about my mother, and to find Alpha's father, but none of it had turned out the way I wanted. I no longer cared what would happen when that clock counted its way down to zero, I just wanted to be somewhere else. Preferably without prior knowledge of what was going to be happening very soon.

Maybe I could be sitting on the lawn outside the college refectory, sharing fruit soys with Alpha, back when all I had to worry about was the fact I'd just enrolled in a Literature class.

Instead I was walking down a plasteel half-cylinder towards . . . well, who knew what?

Alpha was by my side, but she had descended into silence . . . probably unable to believe that her father was a part of this vast conspiracy too.

I knew what followed from that discovery, and felt her pain. Her father had lied to her as well.

I took Alpha's hand in mine as we moved closer to

whatever awaited us at the end of the tunnel.

Already I could see the first hints of our destination. We were approaching the outer edges of an odd, pallid-blue, bioluminescent half-light, and I wondered how long we had left before the digits on that infernal timer behind us counted down to 00.00.

So this is progress, I thought grimly. *You get to see the precise moment that future hits. You're able to see what's coming.* And as Kyle Straker once said: *Nothing good.*

I thought of everything that had happened to us today, each event and discovery, the trail of breadcrumbs that had led to this subterranean world. And that made me remember the story of Theseus that my mother had told me and I realised that – even as she was reading it to me – she had been aware of the tunnels and caverns beneath her.

Had she drawn a secret pleasure from knowing that she had a labyrinth all of her own beneath the house?

Well, I was in that labyrinth now, and at its centre two monsters had been waiting for me.

My parents. My own flesh and blood.

-15-

File: *113/50/05/wtf/Continued*

Source: *LinkData\LinkDiary\Peter_Vincent\Personal*

<LinkDiary Running>

The sickly blue light was an artificial sun for the things that grew underneath it.

At the end of the tunnel was another crater, a pit sunk even deeper into the earth.

Deeper and deeper into the underworld.

The geography of despair.

Where tunnels led on to craters led on to tunnels led on to more craters.

This one was vast. The size of two sports fields at least.

A forest of colossal, pink, fern-like structures pressed tightly together, filling the whole area, with cables and wires entering into the pulsing biomass that sat below the fronds.

There had to be millions of the things in there.

I was looking at my father's neural forest. It had been weird enough hearing about it at the Keynote – although my memories of that were sketchy at best – but seeing it in the flesh was truly, profoundly disturbing. A storage and processing device made entirely from living tissue. In effect: an artificial brain.

We stood on the lip of the pit, bathed in the pale light, and my mother stood back, letting us soak up the sight.

I could see that the ferns of the structure were swaying in unison, as if stirred by a breeze. But there was no breeze down here. The neural forest moved, and it moved by itself.

'This is the MindFeather,' my mother said, and there was wonderment in her voice.

Wonderment and something else.

Pride.

'A network of interconnected minds. Each growth, each feather of the brain, is fractal: a geometrical shape that endlessly repeats down to the tiniest level. If you were to magnify a single branch, then you would see exact self-similarity — another branch, identical to the larger one. Magnify that one, and you would see that it repeats, down and down to the microscopic level, utterly identical.'

'What does it do?' Alpha asked.

'It thinks. It holds information. It is the engine of victory. It is, ultimately, our salvation.'

'Yeah, and it makes toast,' I said. 'But what is it really? What is its purpose?'

My mother joined us at the edge of the crater.

'With every upgrade, everything that we are is altered by a signal from *somewhere else*,' she said. 'We have had no success in tracing that signal's origin, and we have no idea what kind of creatures may be transmitting it.

'It didn't take long for The Straker Committee to confirm that aliens were interfering in human affairs. There is evidence all around us. The existence of the Link was our strongest example. Kyle Straker told us that the creatures were using the human race as some kind of data storage. The storage units had to be connected somehow.

'That's the true secret behind the Link. It is nothing more

than a by-product of our necessary connectivity. It is a symbol of the power that enslaves us. And, ironically, it is our connectivity that will save us.

'This neural forest is upgrade-proof; it exists in a state of deep hypnosis. It was designed to provide a massive memory that would not be affected by any future modifications to the human operating system.

'But it has also been programmed with the history of, and the specific code for, every past upgrade.

'Every MindFeather is aware of the different versions of human existence, stretching back to the earliest software.

'In just under twenty minutes, the human race will be upgraded. This is unstoppable. We do not have the technology, nor the understanding, to disrupt the coming signal.

'But this upgrade will not go the same way that all the others have. We might not be able to stop it, but we are now – for the first time in human history – in a position to make it happen on our own terms.'

'You're going to interfere with it,' Alpha said, her voice shocked.

My mother shrugged.

'We will no longer tolerate the interference of others in human affairs,' she said proudly. 'That was the decision of the committee. There is a period in human development where the child outgrows the parent. We have reached that point.'

'What have you done?' I asked.

'We have made sure that this upgrade does not go as they intend. Running computer code adapted from the code in the silos, we are going to disrupt it. We have taught the fractal forests to resist and we are going to broadcast that resistance – via the Link – into the minds of every man, woman and child on planet Earth. We are confident that we will cause a fatal error in their process.

'Very few people are going to be in the correct state for the latest upgrade to take. When the MindFeather starts transmitting, the message will be the history of human upgrades. We're going to knock *everyone* back to one of many past software versions. Some will become 1.2. Some will become 0.4. Some will be 1.0. Just about everyone on the planet is going to be left behind.'

'To what end?' I asked, horrified by what she was telling us. 'What can you *possibly* hope to gain?'

'Only everything,' my mother said, as if I was a total idiot and it was beneath her to have to explain it to me. 'Can you imagine what our programmers might look like? The things that we would learn if we were to meet them? Can you even begin to comprehend how utterly different to us they must be? They must be to us as we are to amoebas. We might as well call them gods.'

My mother's voice became quiet and reverential.

'Well, we intend to see the face of God.'

Flashes of my nightmare came back, and I kept seeing those terrible creatures pressed against the skin of the sky.

Who said they even have faces? I thought grimly.

'What are you talking about?' Alpha's voice rose. 'How will *this* allow you to see the face of God?'

'It's so easy,' my mother said. 'The people of Earth are nothing more than an organic computer to them. If a computer breaks down – if it freezes or crashes – what does a person do? Peter, your LinkPad suffers a fatal crash, what do *you* do?'

I thought about it. She couldn't mean . . . She couldn't . . . It was insane.

'I'd call out a tech guy,' I said, feeling the weight of the idea expanding within me, chilling and inescapable.

'Exactly,' she said. 'When planet Earth malfunctions, they're going to send out their technical support department.

'And we are going to be waiting for them.'

-16-

File: *113/50/05/wtf/Continued*

Source: *LinkData\LinkDiary\Peter_Vincent\Personal*

<LinkDiary Running>

She grinned.

I had a clenched fist in place of a stomach, and the thoughts in my head were dark and ugly.

'That's your whole plan?' I asked her. 'You intend to lure *aliens* down to Earth to repair their *computer*?'

The tone of my voice made my mother narrow her eyes.

'Don't you see?' she said. 'We're going to end this, once and for all.'

'Oh, you're going to end it all right,' I said. 'But what makes you think they'll want to fix us?'

'What?'

'Sending out technical support is only one solution for them. But the last time I broke a LinkPad — when I dropped it on a slider and watched it smash to pieces at my feet — do you know what I did? I decided it wasn't worth repairing, and I bought a new model. Shinier, with more features.' My anger took over. 'Your whole plan hinges on some mighty big assumptions,' I pretty much shouted at her. 'That they will think that coming here will be viable; and that there are no other races in the universe that they can use as the latest, shinier, model. How can you be so sure?'

The question hung there in the air like a tangible thing.

My mother suddenly looked uncomfortable as my words sank in. 'Even if they don't come we will be free of them . . .'

'Really?' Alpha interrupted. 'Peter, what happened to your old LinkPad?'

'It was recycled,' I said. 'Broken up for its components, and then melted down.'

Alpha nodded.

'It's David Vincent's fatal flaw,' she explained. 'It always has been. He has tunnel vision. He sees one way forward and pursues it. And that leads to the Law of Unintended Consequences.

'Our first discussion.' She turned to me and smiled. 'Our first point of similarity.'

Already I could see my mother's face had completely altered, from superior, haughty pride to immediate concern.

'He invented an artificial honey bee and then stood by and watched as the last real bees died out,' Alpha said, 'when he should have targeted the mite that was killing them. His ideas are so bold, so *clever*, so *visionary* that people kind of forget to question them. They get so wrapped up in them, in his sureness, in his arrogant certainty, that they forget that he might not be right.

'You really should have questioned this one, Mrs Vincent. I suspect that this time he's gone one better than killing off the bees. This time he might just have killed us all.'

-17-

File: *113/50/05/wtf/Continued*

Source: *LinkData\LinkDiary\Peter_Vincent\Personal*

<LinkDiary Running>

My mother looked at Alpha like she was genuinely seeing her for the first time. Her belief in what she was doing had suddenly melted away. Then her face hardened.

'How do we stop it?' I demanded.

'Stop it?' My mother looked aghast. 'Peter, you can't.'

'What I can't do is trust that things will turn out the way you *hope* they will,' I told her.

'It's too late.'

'It hasn't happened yet, Mrs Vincent,' Alpha said. 'So it can't be too late. How do we stop it?'

My mother looked dazed, and I felt a moment's pity for her.

'The computers . . .' she said. 'The neural forest . . . it's a big circuit . . .'

'How do we disrupt it?'

'There's no time . . .'

'HOW DO WE DISRUPT IT?'

'The computers . . .'

'We destroy them?'

My mother stared back at me. I shook my head in frustration.

'If we destroy the computer, will it stop this from happening?' I demanded.

'I – I don't know.' she looked lost. 'David is controlling the whole thing . . . the neural interface . . .'

Alpha said: 'She must mean all those wires that he was applying to his head.'

I nodded.

Guess it meant that we had to stop HIM; we had to stop my father.

-18-

File: *113/50/05/wtf/Continued*

Source: *LinkData\LinkDiary\Peter_Vincent\Personal*

<LinkDiary Running>

We ran back down the tunnel, Alpha and I, leaving my mother standing in the glow of the neural forest, looking lost.

A week ago I would have given anything to see her again, now I was relieved to be leaving her. Dreams so often become nightmares. Family can so easily become foes. And people are always more stupid than you give them credit for.

We reached the first crater and the countdown had already reached 12.42. Just seeing it up there on the clock made me feel sick.

'Do we have a plan?' Alpha asked, out of breath and puffing hard.

'Stop him,' I said.

'That's a goal,' Alpha said. 'Not a plan. A plan would tell us how we were going to achieve it.'

She was right, of course.

I looked around me. 'These wires,' I said. 'These wires and cables. They're everywhere.'

'If you're thinking about pulling them all out,' Alpha said, 'then we have ourselves a bona fide plan.' She gave a huge smile, leaned in and kissed me.

'For luck,' she whispered.

'See you on the other side,' I said, and then we got to work.

-19-

File: *113/50/05/wtf/Continued*

Source: *LinkData\LinkDiary\Peter_Vincent\Personal*

<LinkDiary Running>

I grabbed a handful of the cables nearest me and pulled. They were connected to the back of one of the computer banks, and looked pretty important.

There was a horrible second where I felt no give at all, but then I put more shoulder into it and they tore loose of their housings with such ease that I fell over, clutching the wires to my chest.

That's done it, I thought. I dropped the cables, got to my feet and moved to the next computer. I heard Alpha tearing wires free from somewhere nearby and grinned.

I was pulling a second bunch free when an alert

sounded somewhere close by, loud and metallic.

That's REALLY done it, I thought.

I yanked the wires, but these ones really didn't feel like they wanted to be torn out. I pulled and pulled, but was getting nowhere.

I wrapped them around my arms to brace them, leaned back until all of my weight was concentrated on the wires, and finally they started to tear away from the computer.

'COME ON!' I said through gritted teeth. In desperation I threw myself backwards, and then I was on the floor again, with another bunch of useless wires in my hands.

'YES!' I cried triumphantly, feeling like maybe we DID have a chance of stopping this mad plan of my father's; and it was then that I saw the white-coated technician standing above me, looking down with anger in his eyes.

I recognised him, of course.

It was Perry Knight's dad.

Parents.

Again with the parents.

Was there anyone's dad who *wasn't* involved in this?

'What are you doing here, Peter?' Mr Knight asked me,

although it was obvious from his voice that he already knew the answer: he started edging closer to me.

'You're in on this lunacy too?' I asked him, and was about to get up, but he moved too quickly, bringing his foot up and bringing it down again on my right arm. He kept it there, putting his weight behind it, and for a moment there was a red flash behind my eyes, as the pain hit home.

Hard.

And then he ground his heel into my arm for good measure.

It was madness! This was Perry's dad, who'd bounced me on his knee when I was still small enough to be bounced; who'd taken me out on family trips when Perry begged him hard enough; who'd babysat me when my father was called away.

A man who was now trying to break my arm.

My eyes were half closed in pain but I could just see Alpha out of the corner of my eye, creeping towards Mr Knight until she was right behind him. I let out a primal roar and rolled my body so that it smacked right into his shins. The pain was intense, but I kept pushing and eventually he stepped backwards. It released my arm – after he ground it underfoot once more – and then the backs of his legs made contact with Alpha's hunched frame and he toppled over her, going down like he'd just been shot.

I tried my best to ignore the pain, but something in my arm had been badly hurt and I made a pretty poor show of getting to my feet. Mr Knight was already half up, and he was going to beat me to it, there was no doubt.

But he hadn't counted on Alpha.

She turned her body and swung her elbow back, fast and hard, until it connected with Mr Knight's rising face. The force of the blow sent blood spraying out of his nose and his eyes rolled back into his head.

He was out cold.

Alpha moved quickly, grabbing a skein of wires and wrapping them around Mr Knight's ankles.

'You OK?' she barked as she pulled the wires tight and knotted them, before passing them up his back and using them to secure his hands.

'He almost broke my arm,' I said, getting slowly to my feet. 'That was one hex of a rescue. Thank you.'

Alpha inspected her handiwork, gave the wires a good hard pull for luck, then dusted her hands off.

'No one beats up on my Kyle paradigm without answering to me,' she said, and then nodded towards the geodesic dome. 'What say we go and break up your father's little control centre?'

I just nodded in reply and raced after her.

-20-

File: *113/50/05/wtf/Continued*

Source: *LinkData\LinkDiary\Peter_Vincent\Personal*

<LinkDiary Running>

The length of metal tubing was right where I'd dropped it, just outside the dome. The pain in my arm had developed into a grinding, throbbing sensation and there was no way I could pick up anything, so I pointed to it and Alpha bent down and retrieved it for me.

'I'll keep him busy,' I said. 'You . . . you just smash up everything in sight. The more expensive looking, the better.'

'Was that a plan?' Alpha joked. 'Did you just formulate another actual PLAN?'

I tried to smile but it probably looked more like a grimace.

Then we headed to the entrance of the dome.

My father hadn't thought he needed to close it up again, and we walked straight in through the opening. Another piece of evidence, if more was needed, of his poor judgment.

He had his back to us, and his head was festooned with wires. He was studying the screens and didn't hear us coming in. Alien code flowed across one screen, always in motion.

I approached my father, holding my right arm crossed across my chest, the hand resting on my left shoulder. I heard the first of Alpha's blows with the pipe, and so did he.

He turned, a look of surprise on his face. When he saw me and Alpha, surprise quickly changed to fury.

'What the —' he began, but I was already bending at the waist, aiming my left shoulder at his midriff and charging straight at him.

He raised a feeble hand to fend me off but my momentum was good enough that I connected with him. Hard. He had a computer console behind him and his spine hit the edge with quite some force.

He let out a dull 'oof' and then my good hand was reaching up and I got a handful of the wires that were attached to his head.

The side of his hand hit me between the eyes, making my vision go starry, but the wires finally came loose.

He let out a scream of anger, and then his defence mechanisms must have kicked in because he suddenly managed to get the meat of his hand under my chin and started pushing.

My head went back sharply before his other hand found my wounded arm and started to squeeze.

'You stupid fool,' he growled. 'You'll ruin everything.'

I felt the pain starting to overwhelm me, felt the raw redness threaten to consume me.

'I really hope so, Dad,' I said.

I could hear that Alpha was making the most of the distraction to really lay into the equipment around her. Glass was breaking and metal clanging. My father pushed me aside and lurched towards her, his hands outstretched into rigid claws of rage. It looked like he had murder in his eyes.

I clenched my teeth, let out a roar of my own, threw my arms out to grab his legs.

And missed.

I fell heavily on my injured arm and felt a terrible flash of pain through my entire body.

I saw my father reaching Alpha.

My mind screamed at my body to get up and help her out, but my body just wouldn't obey.

We haven't done enough, I thought, and knew then that all was lost.

-21-

File: *113/50/05/wtf/Continued*

Source: *LinkData\LinkDiary\Peter_Vincent\Personal*

<LinkDiary Running>

I was utterly helpless and could only watch on as my father grabbed hold of Alpha's shoulders and threw her aside. She bounced off some machinery and hit the ground, letting out a little whimper of pain.

I think if I could have, I would have killed him.

'You can't stop this,' my father said, and the expression on his face was both crazed and euphoric. 'No one can stop it. Least of all a pair of stupid children.'

'Please don't do this!' Alpha yelled. 'What if you're wrong?'

My father glared down at her with contempt.

'The last thing I need is advice from you,' he snarled.

'Stay down there, where you belong, and watch the future dawn.'

I didn't even know that I had deployed my filaments until I felt them connect with the input panel on the computer I was lying next to. I looked up and saw them stretching further than I had ever extended them before, at least a metre.

My father spotted them as they interfaced with the computer panel.

'What are you doing, Peter?' he asked, a mocking tone in his voice.

I didn't know. I mean I didn't consciously send them out of my hand, and I had absolutely no idea what to do now that they were there.

And then it happened.

The Link was suddenly alive in my mind, but not like it ever had been before.

Millions of voices suddenly invaded my head, the Link turned up to extreme, overwhelming me with its chatter. I heard music and traffic reports, news stories and diary entries, secrets and lies and hopes and dreams and fears. And I heard them all at the same time, bruising my mind with their sheer volume. I felt them building up like a mad pressure inside my skull, a skull that was surely going to burst from all that information.

I opened my mouth to scream, just to release some of the pressure, but no sound came out. Instead I felt that pressure converted into data; felt the data pass through my body into my hand; and then I felt it disperse outwards through my filaments.

I unloaded the Link into the computer.

'Take that!' I shouted.

And nothing happened.

Nothing at all.

-22-

File: 113/50/05/wtf/Continued

Source: LinkData\LinkDiary\Peter_Vincent\Personal

<LinkDiary Running>

I lay there, trembling and drained, with a head that felt like it was about to explode, and still the countdown to our extinction ticked away, second by terrible second.

'Well?' my father asked, 'What was that about?'

I didn't have a clue. For a moment or two then it had been as if I was *channelling* some energy, or something, and I had allowed myself to feel hope.

But nothing was going to save us.

My father started laughing.

Laughing at me. I looked over at Alpha. She started to give me a wan smile, and then stopped halfway through it.

Her head moved from side to side, and then I saw the smile develop into a massive grin. And she started laughing too.

I thought she had lost her mind, and it even stopped my father. He looked down at her, puzzled.

Alpha pulled herself together, but was still grinning.

'Listen,' she said triumphantly.

So I did.

Then I retracted my filaments.

And started laughing myself.

-23-

File: *113/50/05/wtf/Continued*

Source: *LinkData\LinkDiary\Peter_Vincent\Personal*

<LinkDiary Running>

'What's that?' my father asked, although he of all people should have recognised the sound.

As it got closer — and louder, of course — I saw a look of panic settle on to my father's face.

'NO!' He protested. 'This is . . . it can't be . . . WHY?'

I was thinking about symmetry and neatness, about how it felt like my life was running along hidden tracks beneath my feet, and about the odd connections that today had shared with the crazy dream I'd had. In that kind of mental environment nothing comes as a surprise any more.

THEY got closer.

And closer.

Until their ferocious buzzing was unmistakable.

Bees.

And, by the sound of it: MILLIONS of them.

They were thundering through the air, through the underground complex, towards us, and they were so loud that I felt a moment's fear myself.

The stings that a small swarm of them had inflicted had been bad enough.

This swarm was something different entirely.

A deafening buzz.

Oh, and you programmed them to be so fast, didn't you? I thought.

And then the buzzing sound drowned out even my own thoughts, and metal bodies pinged and smashed and scraped against the shell of the dome.

Alpha had made her way over to me and she took my hand in hers and looked at me with wonderment. She said something, but even though her mouth was less than twenty centimetres from my ear, her words were buried beneath the noise.

Suddenly the dome was breached, and the bees poured in. Relentless and unstoppable, within seconds the air was thick with them.

My father was waving his arms in some mad dumb show, but the bees ignored him, ignored me, ignored Alpha, and they went straight for the computer terminals.

Like sentient bullets they smashed into the equipment. Unlike bullets, however, they could go back for another go.

And another.

And then another.

Metal rang against metal, and the loudest sound I had ever heard became louder still. I felt Alpha's hand clench tighter on to mine, and I realised that if the bees decided to turn their attentions our way then we were dead.

No doubt.

But it seemed as if they had no interest in us at all.

Metal casings buckled under their relentless onslaught.

Monitors smashed.

And still the bees attacked.

Within the space of a mere twenty seconds or so they had managed to batter their way into the hearts of the computers, and then they turned their fury on to the innards: chipsets and capacitors; logic boards and quantum chips.

Sparks flared, became flames, and soon smoke was pouring from the computers. It wasn't long before it became a dense cloud that made my eyes water and my throat sting.

Through the smoke, and the thick cloud of bees, I could vaguely see my father. He stood there, waving his arms and swatting at the invading army, as if he stood any chance at all of repelling them.

They ignored him.

He was irrelevant.

I turned to Alpha, then we got up from the floor, ignored the storm of metal creatures around us, and made for the door of the dome.

-24-

File: *113/50/05/wtf/Continued*

Source: *LinkData\LinkDiary\Peter_Vincent\Personal*

<LinkDiary Running>

Outside the dome the air was fresher.

A little, anyway.

At least it didn't make me feel sick to breathe.

I was struggling to find a part of me that didn't hurt. My arm throbbed, my neck ached, my eyes were streaming and felt like they were full of grit, the bridge of my nose hurt, and I don't know how many bee stings I was still carrying from earlier, but they had decided to start screaming out now too.

I looked back and saw that the flames within the geodesic dome were really hitting their stride, and black smoke was billowing from its entrance.

I grinned in spite of myself, then a hand mussed my hair and I looked at Alpha standing there, right by my side. She looked a little frazzled, with smoky marks on her face, but she returned the grin.

Then I looked up to the doomsday clock: 08.57.

'I'll love you to the end of the world,' I muttered, immediately regretting it.

'Not good enough,' Alpha said, smiling. 'I'm needy. Something trifling like the end of the world is not a good enough excuse for you to stop calling.'

My father had finally given up on trying to save his precious project from destruction at the hands – or should that be wings? – of another of his precious projects. He emerged from the dome looking worse than I felt, with black smoke-marks staining his face.

He looked small and diminished.

'The bees . . .' he said incredulously. 'I don't understand.'

'I connected with your computer terminal and told the bees that your whole network was an unauthorised intruder.'

'How the hex did you do that?'

I shrugged. 'It's a little hazy,' I said.

'This isn't the only complex like this.' It sounded like my father was trying to convince himself, rather than us. 'You may have destroyed my work here, but it goes on around the world. You have achieved nothing.'

'We'll see,' I said, 'in eight minutes or so.'

'Why did you do this?' my father asked, and he sounded like he genuinely had no idea.

For the smartest man I knew, he was also the stupidest.

'Because you didn't kill the mites,' I said and he looked at me like I was insane.

He shook his head.

'Millgrove was important, but not vital,' he said. 'You and your girlfriend here just destroyed millions of credits worth of equipment and started a couple of fires, but that's it.'

'At least we gave it a pretty good try,' Alpha said.

'In eight minutes it won't matter,' my father said. 'Things are going to change, one way or the other.'

'Things always change,' Alpha said. 'It's what you do when it does that's important.'

He gave us a really ugly smile. 'If you DID succeed in

ruining thirty years of work then the only thing you've won is another upgrade. In eight minutes you'll be monsters.'

I hadn't thought of that. I'd been so caught up in stopping him, I hadn't really had time to consider what would happen if we actually succeeded.

My father saw the realisation as it dawned on my face. 'I wonder if you'll even remember each other,' he said spitefully. 'Anyway, you haven't got much time, Peter. You'd better get started.'

'Started?' I had no idea what the hex he was talking about.

'Obey the paradigm,' my father said.

'What does that EVEN mean?'

'Every upgrade has a Kyle and it has a Lilly,' my father said. 'Don't ask me why. It's the way things *always* are. We call them paradigms, but you could call them archetypes, or echoes, it doesn't matter. The Lilly paradigm follows her Kyle into the fire.'

'And what does the Kyle paradigm do?'

'You already know the answer to that one, my son. He leaves behind a record.'

'You want me to write this down?' I said mockingly.

'I don't want anything from you,' he said, turning his back on us.

'What you were doing was *wrong*, Mr Vincent,' Alpha said.

'I guess we'll find out soon enough,' he said and started to walk away.

I leaned on Alpha and we went to follow him, but he turned around and pointed down one of the tunnels.

'There's some storerooms in a corridor off the side of Tunnel 3. You might find something there you can use.'

'Use for what?' I asked him.

'Playing out your role,' he said and then started up the ladder.

-25-

File: *113/50/05/wtf/Continued*

Source: *LinkData\LinkDiary\Peter_Vincent\Personal*

<LinkDiary Running>

Discussion took about ten seconds. It wasn't as if we were exactly spoiled for choices.

'You do realise that my father is quite mad?' I said.

'Mad or not, I think someone should make some sort of a record of what happened here today,' Alpha said.

'You want to spend the last few minutes we've got left obeying my father's stupid paradigm theory?'

'It's either that or sit here and wait.'

We made our way across the crater and I looked up to the silos towering above us. There were more 'ghosts' gathered around them, some of them kneeling, all of them staring intently at the concrete structures.

I was about to turn away when I saw that one of them was looking our way.

My mother.

She raised her hand in acknowledgment, and I gave her a solemn nod.

Then I noticed a figure standing next to her.

An old man with a mane of black hair.

The man I'd seen and heard just after my LinkDiary crashed; who had been shouting about memories and holes. The man I'd thought was a goblin man from the poem my mother had read to me, and who'd later appeared in a dream and delivered just enough vague and cryptic clues to lead us here.

Here he was, standing next to her, by the silos.

I thought again of invisible connections that linked everything together. I thought about tech-guys and alien programmers and how they might be a little more clever than my father had given them credit for when it came to fixing systems that were *going* to be a problem.

Maybe they would fix things *before* they got out of hand.

Maybe they had already been, done the job, and gone.

I looked at the man and he made a circle with his thumb and forefinger.

I wasn't sure if it was an 'OK' sign, or a snake eating its own tail.

I decided that it really didn't matter.

I gave a replica of the symbol back, and then we hurried down the tunnel.

epilogue

File: *224/09/12fin*

Source: *LinkData\LinkDiary\Live\Peter_Vincent\Personal*

<RUN>

It's starting.

Alpha and I are walking back down the tunnel towards the silos, and I don't know whether it's the contact lenses, or our imaginations, but the air is thick with the alien code. It bristles on our skin like heat rash.

We are hand in hand and I'm carrying the flash drive, recording live on to it, just in case it captures something that will be useful, next time around.

Assuming there will be a next time.

I can't stop thinking about my father, and his crazy plan, and the way that his own bees proved to be his downfall.

How did I do that, exactly?

Convince the bees that my father's computers were a threat that needed to be eradicated?

I mean I'm not even 100% certain that's what happened, but it just kind of feels like that's what I did.

I am sure that I didn't deploy my filaments to connect with the computer. I remember feeling shocked when I felt them touch the metal input panel.

So what happened, exactly?

The only thing that I can think of is my feelings when I saw the goblin man standing on the ridge above us, next to my mother.

What if someone else – something else – had been guiding my hand?

Maybe the tech-guys my father had so wanted to see for himself had pre-empted him. Used me to do their dirty work for them.

Is that even possible?

Because if they are capable of such actions, why didn't they stop him before? I mean there is such a thing as cutting things too fine.

Unless . . .

Unless they wanted something.

Too many questions will never find answers, I guess.

But I don't feel afraid now; I don't know why.

Maybe it's that I'm with Alpha, and whatever happens, happens to us together.

Whether my father's plan to see the face of God succeeds, or whether he has doomed us all, or whether this will be just another upgrade that we don't even know happened . . . we're going to be finding out about now.

I wonder if anyone will ever discover this record. If they do, I hope they don't bookend it with editor's notes like the Straker Tapes.

The alien language is everywhere now.

There is a sound in the air, a static crackle, and then a wave of . . . something . . . hits us.

Hot and electric and

<LinkDiary Crashing>

<Read/Write Error>

@ξ^*($*23KJLKASDLKJSSeawiuro9034028140eria[po-/sdjf

hgasd/90452poweiqwifadslkfasderqntveexndfa

DFJKKEWLRQNWDXSXDSCkjdsflsflfeoiwr98998989888 ****

))))l`kdfsjadlfewr

<LinkDiary Off>

Heisenberg University

Professor Lucas Whybrow
Professor of WorldBrain Studies

My colleagues think me mad.

They point to the fact that we are still here, that the WorldBrain contains no other records like this, that I have been working too hard, that there is no evidence for any of the events Peter Vincent describes, and they have chosen to paint me as the victim of an elaborate hoax.

I know that it sounds incredible. But still, I believe in Peter Vincent. Amalfi Del Rey. Millgrove. Kyle Straker.

Even if I am the only one who does, it is enough.

I have been removed from duties at the University. It was when I pointed out the similarities between the WorldBrain and the 'neural forest' that Peter described that the department heads started to worry about me.

Maybe, I argued, the MindFeather WAS our WorldBrain. Maybe that was the sole purpose of the David Vincent project. The REAL purpose.

Maybe our alien programmers WANTED him to create it. Maybe it was a hardware upgrade that was required BEFORE the software could be installed this time.

It would provide answers to the questions that Peter was asking just before the upgrade hit and his story was silenced.

The WorldBrain is integral to everything we do. It is a living organism that dreams up new technologies, new philosophies, new structures and systems, new solutions to age-old problems. It has changed the way we think about ourselves, and the way we behave towards each other.

I am on an extended leave of absence. I suppose I should

be working on regaining my reputation, on putting the Vincent archive behind me, but I can't. Everything else seems pointless compared to the data.

I have copied the files and I spend most of my time trying to rebuild the damaged sectors, to find out what was lost in that final, critical shutdown.

Is the actual, physical experience of being upgraded contained in those few, scrambled lines of data?

If it is I will decode it.

I must know.

My colleagues call it madness.

Me, I call it faith .

Also by
MIKE LANCASTER

'My name is Kyle Straker.
And I don't exist anymore.

So begins the story of Kyle Straker,
recorded on to audio tapes.
You might think these tapes are a
hoax. But perhaps they contain the
history of a past world.

If what the tapes say are true,
it means that everything we think
we know is a lie.

And if everything we know is a lie
does that mean that we are, too?

PLUG INTO A GRIPPING
NEW GENERATION OF SCI-FI

EGMONT PRESS: ETHICAL PUBLISHING

Egmont Press is about turning writers into successful authors and children into passionate readers – producing books that enrich and entertain. As a responsible children's publisher, we go even further, considering the world in which our consumers are growing up.

Safety First
Naturally, all of our books meet legal safety requirements. But we go further than this; every book with play value is tested to the highest standards – if it fails, it's back to the drawing-board.

Made Fairly
We are working to ensure that the workers involved in our supply chain – the people that make our books – are treated with fairness and respect.

Responsible Forestry
We are committed to ensuring all our papers come from environmentally and socially responsible forest sources.

For more information, please visit our website at www.egmont.co.uk/ethical

Egmont is passionate about helping to preserve the world's remaining ancient forests. We only use paper from legal and sustainable forest sources, so we know where every single tree comes from that goes into every paper that makes up every book.

This book is made from paper certified by the Forestry Stewardship Council (FSC®), an organisation dedicated to promoting responsible management of forest resources. For more information on the FSC, please visit **www.fsc.org**. To learn more about Egmont's sustainable paper policy, please visit **www.egmont.co.uk/ethical**.